GUILTY

Norah
McClintock

ORCA BOOK PUBLISHERS

Library and Archives Canada Cataloguing in Publication

McClintock, Norah
Guilty / Norah McClintock.

Issued also in electronic formats.
ISBN 978-1-55469-989-6

I. Title.
PS8575.C62G83 2012   JC813'.54   C2011-907708-6

First published in the United States, 2012
Library of Congress Control Number: 2011943677

Summary: After Finn's stepmother is allegedly murdered by Lila's father,
the two teens must work together to see what is true. And who is guilty.

*Orca Book Publishers is dedicated to preserving the environment and has printed this book
on paper certified by the Forest Stewardship Council®.*

Orca Book Publishers gratefully acknowledges the support for its publishing
programs provided by the following agencies: the Government of Canada through
the Canada Book Fund and the Canada Council for the Arts, and the Province of British
Columbia through the BC Arts Council and the Book Publishing Tax Credit.

Design by Teresa Bubela
Cover image by Getty Images

ORCA BOOK PUBLISHERS
PO Box 5626, Stn. B
Victoria, BC Canada
V8R 6S4

ORCA BOOK PUBLISHERS
PO Box 468
CUSTER, WA USA
98240-0468

www.orcabook.com
Printed and bound in Canada.

15 14 13 12   •   4 3 2 1

One
FINN

I hear my dad bellow, "What do you think you're doing?" But it's Tracie's voice, sharp and shrill, that pulls me away from my computer.

"Robert," she shrieks. "Do something!"

Robert is my dad, but Tracie is the only one who ever calls him that. To everyone else, he's just Rob.

I go to the window, wondering for the zillionth time how he can stand her. She's always telling him to do something or, better, buy her something, and she does it in a voice that's like a dentist's drill. It's so annoying that you'd do anything to make it stop. I know. I've thought about plenty of ways to shut her up.

I look out the window and see Tracie down in front of the garage. The security light makes ugly shadows on her face. She lies about her age to everyone, and that bright light and those shadows make her look even older than she really is.

She's with my dad, but they aren't alone. There's someone else down there. A man. His back is to me, so I have no idea who he is or what he's doing there. The three of them are just standing in front of the garage—the man with his back to me; Tracie, in the light, her eyes on the man; and my dad, between Tracie and the man.

My dad shouts. It sounds like, "Hey!" Suddenly both he and the man are in motion. My dad lunges at the man. He claws at him, as if he's trying to wrestle something away from him. What's going on? Are they serious, or are they clowning around? Is the man a friend of my dad's? What's he doing here so late?

Tracie shrieks, "Be careful, Robert!" The panic in her voice puts me on full alert. My dad and the man aren't just fooling around. At least, Tracie doesn't seem to think they are. I've decided that maybe I should go down there when:

Blam!

Blam!

I freeze. What the—?

Down below me, Tracie crumples and falls to the ground. My dad turns to look at her. He bellows. He lunges at the man again.

Blam!

Blam!

A second person falls to the ground.

Only my dad is left standing.

I run downstairs and fly out the back door. My dad hears me coming. He spins around. He yells at me, "Call nine-one-one. Call nine-one-one."

I swing back toward the house, duck inside and grab the cordless phone from the kitchen counter. I make the call. I give our address, our phone number, my name. I answer questions. I promise to stay put.

But I don't.

When I finish the call, I run back outside.

My dad is on his knees beside Tracie. His hand is pressed against the side of her neck.

"Dad?"

When he looks at me, I see astonishment in his eyes.

"I—I think she's dead. I—that man, he—" He can't get the words out. He can't finish his sentence.

"It's okay, Dad," I say. "I saw what happened."

My dad doesn't answer. He doesn't move. He must be in shock.

"An ambulance is coming," I say. "The police too." I'm just guessing on that, but it's a safe bet. I mean, I told the 9-1-1 operator that two people had been shot.

"Dad, you should come inside and sit down." I'm afraid if he doesn't, he'll collapse. I take his arm. That's when I finally see the man's face.

"I know him," I say.

My dad's head whips around.

"I mean, I recognize him. He was here earlier tonight. He asked for you. He must have waited for you to come home. Who is he, Dad?"

My dad doesn't move for a whole minute. When he finally speaks, his voice is hoarse.

"He's the man who murdered your mother."

I look down at Tracie. I'm as stunned as my dad about what has just happened. I feel bad for Tracie. I really do, even if I never could stand her. But she's not my mother. She's just some woman my dad married after my mother died.

"I'm talking about Mom, Finn," my dad says. "That man—he's the one who murdered Mom. Your real mom."

I look down at the man who lies motionless on the asphalt. I spoke to him earlier when he came to the door asking to see my dad. Now I find out he's the one who shot and killed my mother more than ten years ago?

Two
LILA

I'm in one hell of a bad mood by the fifth or sixth time the doorbell rings. I knew something was up when he left the apartment after supper. He was acting strange, but when I called him on it, he lied to me. He told me to stop worrying so much, nothing was going to happen, he wasn't going to do anything that would get him into trouble. He told me he had some business to take care of. That was hours ago. It's four in the morning. If he's drunk or, worse, if he's on something, I swear that's it. I'll pack my bags and be out of here. All night I've had the feeling that Aunt Jenny was right. I never should have come here.

The doorbell rings again. I unlatch the door and almost rip it off the hinges when I open it. I'm ready to let him have it.

But it isn't him.

It's a man and a woman, both in suits, both grim-looking. The man shows me his ID. He's a cop. Terrific. Three days out—I'm betting that's some kind of record.

"Are you Lila Ouimette?" the woman cop asks.

If she knows enough to ask the question, then she already knows the answer. But I nod anyway.

"Does Louis Ouimette live here?" her partner asks. He says it Lou-*is*, like Louis Armstrong.

"It's Lou-*ee*," I tell him. "And he's not here. If you find him, do me a favor. Tell him I've gone back to Boston." Back to Aunt Jenny, who warned me. *I know he's your father, Lila, but he's been in prison for ten years. That does things to a man. And before that...*

"When was the last time you saw or spoke to your father?" the woman cop asks.

"This morning." I look at the two cops. "What did he do?"

"Is there anyone else here with you, Ms. Ouimette?" the male cop says, his eyes searching through the open door behind me. I feel ashamed at what they're seeing—the shabby ground-floor apartment in a tiny run-down house that is almost more than we can afford. It's nothing like what I'm used to.

"No. I'm here alone. Why?" Something in the way he asks makes me think of all the cop shows I've watched. My imagination kicks in. I tell myself I'm being ridiculous, but the words come out anyway. "Where's my dad? Did something happen to him?"

"I'm sorry to have to tell you this," the woman cop says. "But your father is dead."

My mind blanks out. I'm looking at the woman cop. She's telling me something else. I see her lips move, but I can't hear her. I can't hear anything except the pounding of my heart. It fills my ears. My father is dead? That's not possible.

"There must be some mistake," I say. Now *I* sound like someone straight out of one of those stupid TV shows.

The two cops look steadily at me. There's no mistake.

"What happened?" I ask. "How did he—?"

"He was shot."

Shot?

"How? Who shot him?"

"We're still investigating," the woman cop says. "We're going to need you to identify your father, Lila, unless there's some other family member who can do it."

"I'm it," I say. "I'm his family." Aunt Jenny is my mom's sister. She doesn't think much of my dad. She never did.

"Is there anyone you'd like to call? Anyone you want to come with you?"

I shake my head. "My father and I moved in here a couple of days ago. Before that, I was in Boston. I don't know anyone here."

The woman cop nods. She asks if she and her partner can step inside while I get changed, which is when I remember that I'm wearing flannel pajama bottoms and a ratty old T-shirt. I nod. They come in, and I go to my room to put on some jeans and a sweater. I run a brush through my hair, even though no one cares what I look like. Not under the circumstances.

I lock the door behind me. I ride with the two cops to a morgue. I steel myself for the identification. I tell them, yes, that's him. That's my father. He looks like he's sleeping.

The two cops lead me away from the morgue. They offer me coffee and ask me questions. What has my father been doing since he got out of prison? Who did he associate with? Has he mentioned any names to me?

"What kind of names?"

"People he wanted to get in touch with. People he knew from before."

I shake my head. "He had a job. He worked as a janitor in a building downtown. They set it up for him. That organization that helps people adjust when they get out of prison. He said he wanted us to be a family. He said he wanted to do the right thing by me. How did you say he got shot?"

"We're still investigating," the male cop says again.

"You have no idea who did it? Did someone try to rob him? Because if they did, they picked the wrong guy."

The male cop perks up when I say that.

"What do you mean?"

"Just that he's broke. Everything he had went to first and last months' rent on the apartment. Is that why he got shot—because he didn't have any money to hand over?"

The woman cop exchanges glances with her partner.

"Did he ever mention the name Robert Newsome?" she asks.

Robert Newsome? I get a bad feeling. My fingers and toes tingle.

"No."

"Do you know who Robert Newsome is?" the male cop asks.

Yeah, I know. Supposedly my father broke into Mr. Newsome's house and robbed the place and killed Mrs. Newsome.

I nod.

"Your father didn't mention that he wanted to see Mr. Newsome or talk to him?" the woman cop asks.

"Why would he do that?" I say, as if I can't possibly imagine. I don't think they believe me. If they do, they're lousy cops.

"He wasn't bitter about what happened?" the woman cop asks.

"He told me he didn't do it," I say. "He told me he didn't do any of it."

There they are exchanging glances again. The woman cop's voice is gentle when she speaks again.

"Lila, he took a plea," she says.

I glance at her partner. He's staring stonily at me, and I know what he's thinking: *You need to wake up and smell the coffee, girl, because if you believe a man when he says he didn't do a crime he pleaded guilty to, then you're dreaming.*

And it's true. My father did plead guilty. He did it in exchange for a reduced charge, manslaughter instead of second-degree murder, ten to life and a good shot at parole instead of fifteen to life with life being a real possibility. But he explained that to me too. He said he did it for me.

"Your mother's gone," he said. "I don't know exactly what happened, but I got framed up good. I know I never killed that woman. But if I don't tell them what they want to hear, if I go to trial, I'll lose for sure. I'll never get out. We'll never be a family."

That's what he said.

I look at the male cop and think maybe he's right. Maybe I do need to wake up. Maybe he pleaded to a reduced charge because it was a good deal. Maybe he did it for himself, not for me. Maybe he spent his whole time in there thinking about what he would do when he got out. And maybe what he was thinking about wasn't what he told me he was thinking about.

Focus on the present, plan for the future. That's what he told me every time I went to see him. For him, that meant staying clean and sober for one more day, keeping his head down for one more day, staying out of trouble for one more day, all so that he could get out when he was supposed to and be my father again. For me, it meant doing my schoolwork and pretending that I didn't hear what other people, including Aunt Jenny, said about him. If I did hear, I pretended I didn't care. Every single day. For ten years.

The two cops tell me again that they're sorry for my loss. They get a uniformed cop to drive me back to the apartment. I wait until the sun comes up before I call Aunt Jenny. It's only when I tell her what happened that I begin to cry. Once I start, I can't stop.

Three
FINN

The night lights up. An ambulance arrives, then another. Cop cars arrive—first one, then two, until, in the end, there are half a dozen. The coroner makes an appearance to look at the two bodies. The neighbors all have their lights on. Some of them are out on the street. They cluster together in little groups and talk about what has happened.

Detectives take my dad and me inside. One goes into the living room with my dad. The other one steers me into the kitchen. I try to make myself look as upset as I can so that the cop with me doesn't think I'm some kind of heartless freak. I do it by imagining how I would feel if my dad had been shot instead of Tracie.

The detective sits at the kitchen table. He makes sure that I take a seat facing away from the window so that I can't see what's going on outside.

"What can you tell me about this, Finn?" he says.

"He was here earlier," I say. "The man. He came here. He asked for my dad."

"When was this?"

"Tonight. Late." When I heard the doorbell, I thought maybe my dad had left his keys at the club, that's how late it was. "After eleven. I told him my dad wasn't here. He was at the club."

"The club he owns?"

I nod.

"Were you alone when he came to the door?"

I nod again.

"Tracie—she's my stepmother—she was at the club with Dad."

"What did the man say when you told him your father wasn't here?"

"Nothing."

"He didn't leave a message or a name?"

"No."

"Did he seem upset?"

"No."

"What did he do?"

"Nothing. He went away. At least, I think he did. I didn't watch him or anything." Why would I?

"Then what?"

"What do you mean?"

"What happened after the man left? Tell me everything you can remember, Finn."

"There isn't much to tell. I finished my homework. I fooled around on my computer. I was playing a game on it when I heard my dad and Tracie."

"You heard them?"

"My dad yelled something, and then she yelled something to him. It sounded like something was wrong, so I got up and went to the window to take a look."

"What did he say?"

"He said, 'What do you think you're doing?'"

"And her?"

"She said, 'Do something, Robert.'"

"When you went to the window, what did you see?"

I tell him everything I can remember.

"You say your dad yelled 'Hey!' at the man," the detective said. "Do you have any idea why?"

"The man must have pulled out a gun."

"Must have? Did you see a gun?"

"Well, no. I was up in my room. I couldn't see everything. But the next thing that happened was I heard two shots and Tracie fell to the ground. Then my dad and the man were fighting, and there were two more shots. By the time I got downstairs, the man was on the ground too."

"Then what?"

"My dad said to call nine-one-one. So I did."

He asks me more questions, mostly about what I saw from the window. He writes down what I say. He finishes just before my father appears, holding on to the doorframe as if that's all that's keeping him on his feet.

"Finn, are you okay?" he asks.

The detective who has been questioning me stands up.

"We'll need you both to come in later to make formal statements," he says.

My dad nods, but it seems to me he hasn't heard.

"Tracie," he says, his voice breaking.

I get up and go to him.

"I'm really sorry, Dad."

"That bastard. Why did he have to come back here? Why couldn't he just leave us alone?" Tears are running down his cheeks. I put my arm around him. He collapses against me. The detective is staring at us. I glare at him. We are not on display. This is our house. This is my father's grief. It's private.

"Come on, Dad." I steer him toward the stairs and help him up to his room. He drops down onto his bed. I help him out of his jacket. I tell him to empty his pants pockets, which he does—wallet, coins, a key ring with a small Swiss Army knife attached to it. I tell him I'm going to get his pajamas for him. When I return with them, his head is bowed. His shoulders are rounded. Suddenly I am seven years old again. Suddenly I remember the night my mother died. My dad's questions are good ones. Why *did* he have to come back here? Why couldn't he just leave us alone?

Four
LILA

Aunt Jenny wants me to come home. I tell her no. The rent on the apartment is paid up for two months, and I want to see what happens. I want to understand why my father was shot dead. I want to know, even though I'm afraid that I won't like the explanation.

Aunt Jenny says she'll come up and stay with me. I tell her not to. I tell her I can handle this on my own. I feel like I've been handling it my whole life.

Aunt Jenny used to take me to see my father twice a year, on my birthday and at Christmas. She only did it because that was all I ever asked her for—a visit with my father. As soon as I was old enough to get a job to pay for the bus tickets and to make the bus trip on my own, I started going once a month. I would see my dad in a public visiting room with dozens of other people visiting their fathers or husbands or sons or brothers or boyfriends. Mostly I would tell him about what I was learning in school. He said he liked to hear about that. He said he learned a lot from me.

We talked only once about why he was in prison. That was on my fifteenth birthday. My father gave me a small necklace with a heart on it. I wore it every day after that. I'm still wearing it. He told me, "I don't care what you hear from anyone, Lila. I didn't do it. I didn't kill that woman."

I told him, "I know, Dad."

That was a lie. I didn't know anything of the kind. But I wanted to believe my father. I wanted to believe that he was as good as any other father. I wanted to believe that, if he was in prison, it was all a big mistake. I wanted to believe it even though the whole time he was in there—since I was seven years old—all I ever heard from Aunt Jenny was that he got what he deserved.

When my father was arrested for the murder, Aunt Jenny said, "He's no good. I told your mother that from the get-go. I don't know why she went ahead and married him. He was always drinking or doing drugs. He was in and out of lockup—fighting, trafficking, petty theft, break-and-enters, you name it. I bet you anything he tells the cops he can't remember what happened that night."

And it's true. I talked to his lawyer. I wanted to know what I was getting into when I agreed to live with him after his release. When he got arrested, first he said he didn't do it.

But they got him with the goods right there in his apartment—stuff stolen from the Newsomes' house. So then he said he didn't remember exactly what he was doing the night it happened. He said he took some pills he scored. Someone at work gave them to him. He said he thought maybe he'd been drinking too. Then they told him, *Louis, it doesn't look good for you. We got you dead-to-rights with the goods. We know you know where she lived and that she kept all that stuff in the house. The way we figure it, you broke in thinking you could score some goods to fence. You didn't think she was in the house. Is that it, Louis? She surprised you, right? And you panicked. That's why you shot her, right, Louis? I bet you didn't even mean to do it, did you? But you know how it goes—someone gets killed while you're committing a criminal act, and it's serious. You could go down for life. You don't want that, do you, Louis? Not with that little girl of yours at home, already without a mother. So why don't you do the right thing? Be a man. Own up to what you did.*

And that's exactly what he did.

He made a deal. His lawyer said it was the smart thing to do because the cops didn't have the gun. He said that for all anyone knew, my father might have had a partner who did the shooting. He said he had a shot at reasonable doubt, and the cops knew it. But he also said that with my father's record, it was a crapshoot. He said if my father was smart, he wouldn't want to roll the dice any more than the cops did, so it was better to make a deal. He said that maybe if my father went inside, he could get himself straight. He said with the deal he made, he would be out before I graduated high school. My father agreed. He told me I shouldn't worry about him. He told me I was the important one, not him. He said he wanted me to be strong and do my schoolwork and make something of myself. He said he wasn't proud of himself, but he was already proud of me and he knew I was going to go places.

I didn't go anywhere except to live with Aunt Jenny. And I went to school.

Meanwhile, my father did his time. He went to rehab while he was in there. The days went by slowly, but it felt like we were both making progress. At least, it did when I was sitting across from him at the table in the visiting room. When I was at home with Aunt Jenny or at school, where everyone knew what my father had done, it felt different. Every minute felt like torture, as if it would never end. But it did.

Finally, my father got out.

Now he's dead. His picture is in the newspaper the next morning, which is how I finally find out what happened. The article in the paper says he was shot dead in a struggle with Robert Newsome. It says the second Mrs. Newsome is dead and that my father shot her. It says there was a witness who saw the whole thing, but it doesn't say who that witness is.

It makes me sick to think about it. After all this time, after believing him for all those years, he lied to me when he said he wasn't going to get himself into any trouble. Because what was he doing at the Newsomes' house? Why did he have a gun? Why did he shoot the second Mrs. Newsome?

I was stupid for ever believing him.

Unless he wasn't lying. Unless he was telling the truth.

Is that possible?

Or am I being stupid again?

Five
FINN

I was a kid when my mother died, but I remember it as if it were yesterday.

My dad took me to the club that night. He said he wanted to give my mom a break. They had been arguing a lot. My dad said it was because my mom was tired.

I used to like going to Dad's club. I still do. I like the noise and the action—the music, the musicians, the singers, all the people, the cocktail waitresses, the bartenders. Dad's club isn't one of those massive places with crazy lights and recorded music. He gets real bands in. Blues bands, rock bands, jazz bands, fusion, salsa, world—you name it.

At the end of the night, he always spends an hour in his office doing what he calls the receipts. That means checking how much money the club brought in that night.

His office is in the basement of the club. It's small and cramped and stuffy. It has one small window up high in the wall that he can open to get some fresh air. The window opens onto the alley, and even though it's small, it has bars over it so no one can break in. Sometimes when I was little, I'd sit on the couch in Dad's office and watch him work. But usually I'd play outside in the hall. The hall is long and wide with a smooth floor. It was perfect for riding my trike up and down. It was even better for my remote-control cars.

That night I had my remote-control cars with me. They didn't run very well on the carpets at home, and my mom wouldn't let me play with them on the hardwood floors in the rooms that had no carpets. She was afraid they would scratch the wood. But Dad let me play with them at the club. I had just figured out how to operate two cars at the same time. It wasn't easy, but I could do it. So I had car races. I raced the two cars up and down, up and down. Usually the race ended with one of the cars crashing. Or both of them.

I remember my dad closing the door to his office. He said he had to make an important phone call. It turned out he was calling Mom.

I don't know how long he was in there talking to her. I just know he was there. When he finally came out, he was smiling.

"Your mother says she's feeling a little better," he said. "She had a quiet evening."

He took me upstairs. The club's kitchen was closed, but my dad was hungry. He went into one of the big fridges and took out some ham. He found some bread and mustard. He made us each a ham sandwich with cheese and lettuce. He cut mine into four triangles. We sat on stools at one of the steel counters and ate. Then my dad found some chocolate cake. We each ate a big slice. Finally we headed home.

"Be quiet," my dad said when he unlocked the front door. He frowned when we got inside, and he turned to punch in his code in the brand-new security system he'd had installed so that my mother would feel safe while he was at the club late. "Your mother is probably sleeping. Tiptoe up the stairs. I mean it, Finn. I'll be up in a minute."

I did as my dad said. I tiptoed all the way up the stairs. I started to creep past my parents' room, careful not to wake Mom.

Started to.

Then I stopped.

And screamed.

But I didn't wake my mother. I could have screamed all night and never wakened her. She was lying on the floor. There was red stuff all around her head.

Blood.

I screamed and screamed and screamed. I screamed so much that my father had to hold me tightly to make me stop. I wouldn't let him let me go, not even when he had to go to the police station. I went with him. They got some woman to try to pry me off him. I screamed even louder. But I must have tired myself out, because the next thing I knew, I was sitting beside the woman out in a hallway, waiting for the police to finish talking to my dad.

And now here I am ten years later, sitting in what feels like the exact same place. Sitting and waiting for the cops to finish talking to my dad.

Six
LILA

I don't trust newspapers. They don't always get a story right the first time. So I wait for the two detectives to call and tell me what really happened.

But they don't call.

That's when I decide to go to the police station to talk to them. The sergeant at the desk sends me upstairs, where he says the detectives are. But when I get up there, someone else tells me that they're busy. He says I can wait if I want and shows me where I can sit.

The waiting area is just a row of chairs out in the hall. One other person is sitting there. He looks about my age. His face is pale. He looks tired. But he notices me, even though I sit four chairs away from him. He sort of nods at me. I nod back. Then I look away. I don't feel like talking to anyone.

"Is everything okay?" the guy asks after a few minutes.

I turn my head to see who he's talking to. He's looking at me.

"Is everything okay?" he says again. "I mean, I hope you're not here for anything serious."

"My father died," I say.

That shuts him up. But not for long.

"I saw someone get killed," he says. When I don't say anything, he says, "Are you sure you're okay?"

I want to tell him to leave me alone. Instead, I hear myself say, "How did it happen? The person you saw get killed."

"People," he says, correcting me. "It was people who got killed. Two of them. They were shot."

I know right then that he doesn't know the people. Either that or they don't mean anything to him. He isn't all rattled by seeing them get shot. He doesn't look like he's in shock or that he's been crying. They're just two people.

"That must have been awful," I say.

"My dad's pretty broken up," the guy says. "His wife was one of the victims."

His wife? That's a strange way to put it.

"She wasn't your mother?" I ask.

He shakes his head.

"She was my stepmother. My mother died a long time ago."

"I'm sorry." I really am.

He looks into my eyes.

"The man who was shot—he killed my mom," he says. "My real mom, I mean. Now he's dead. And you know what? I'm glad. And I'm glad I saw it happen."

I don't know what to say. Some people appear in the doorway to the detectives' room. It's a man and the same two detectives who told me that my father is dead. I stare at the man. He looks at the guy sitting near me. The two detectives look at me. The woman detective is frowning.

"Thank you for coming in," she says in a loud voice. "I'm sure you want to get your son back home."

The man nods. He looks a lot more upset than his son. Other than that, he looks exactly like he did in the newspaper clippings I dug up in the library a few years ago. He's Robert Newsome. He is tall and tanned and well-dressed. He has thick black hair and dark-blue eyes. He looks like the TV version of a grieving husband. He nods to his son, who stands up immediately. They walk to the elevator together. The woman detective watches them step into the elevator before she comes over to me.

"What can I do for you, Lila?" she asks.

"You can tell me what they said," I say. I mean Mr. Newsome and the witness, whom I now know is Mr. Newsome's son.

She shakes her head.

"I can't do that. We don't discuss ongoing investigations."

"He was my father."

"I know. And I'm sorry."

"What about the first time?" I ask.

"What do you mean?" she asks.

"What about the first time, when my father went to prison? Can you tell me about that?"

"Didn't your father tell you?"

"I want to know what the police know."

The woman detective glances over her shoulder at her partner. He shrugs, like he doesn't care anything about me or my father. Maybe he's thinking my father got what he deserved. Maybe he thinks I'm just like my father.

"Okay," the woman detective says finally. "Come and sit down. Let me see what I can find out."

She leads me to a small room with a table and two chairs in it and tells me to sit down. I'm guessing that the room is used for questioning people. A few minutes pass. She comes back with a can of pop for me and a file folder.

"I thought you might be thirsty," she says. She sits down at the table and opens the file folder. "Okay, let's see what we have here."

I open the can of pop because she's been nice enough to get it for me. I force myself to take some sips just to be polite. But mostly I listen to her lay out the facts of my father's arrest. I feel myself go numb all over. The case against him was solid. Really solid. And that makes me wonder: why, after all these years, did he go back to Mr. Newsome's house?

Seven
FINN

Everything is a mess that whole day. My dad is completely shell-shocked. He talks to the police. He talks to a lawyer. He talks to Tracie's mom, who is her only living relative. Her mom is in a nursing home. She has Alzheimer's. But my dad calls her anyway. Then he starts in on the funeral arrangements.

"What kind of flowers do you think Tracie would like?" he asks me, as if she is going to be able to smell them and hold them.

"I don't know, Dad."

"She hates lilies." He's talking like she's still alive. "She likes blue. What kind of flowers are blue?" He looks at me again and waits for me to answer. I don't know anything about flowers.

"Why don't you ask the people at the funeral home?" I say.

He doesn't answer. Instead he says, "She needs clothes."

"What are you talking about, Dad?"

"I have to pick out something nice for her to wear. But I don't know what."

I get up. I take him by the arm. I say, "Give me the keys to the car, Dad."

He looks at me like I'm talking to him in a language that he doesn't understand.

"We're going to a funeral home," I say. "We'll talk to someone. They can help you make some decisions." He looks so lost. I shove aside my feelings for Tracie and concentrate on my dad and *his* feelings.

"They should have told you, Dad," I say. "They should have asked you to go there and say something."

He looks more lost than ever.

"Who?" he says.

"The parole board. That's the way it's supposed to work, isn't it? You're supposed to get a say, aren't you?" It's the way it always seems to play out on TV. The family of some murder victim goes to the parole hearing and says their piece and, a lot of the time, parole is denied.

"They gave him parole eligibility after ten years," my dad says wearily. "He served the ten."

"You're still supposed to have a say. The least they could have done was warn you they were letting him out."

"I suppose," he says. "But what's done is done, Finn."

"Yeah, but—"

My dad stifles a sob. I shut my mouth. What am I doing? He's already falling apart. Why am I swinging a hammer at him, shattering him into smaller and smaller pieces?

"Come on, Dad," I say. I hold out my hand. It takes a moment, but he fishes out his key chain with the Swiss Army knife on it.

We go outside and get into my dad's car. I drive to a place on the main street near our house that I've passed a million times on my way to and from school but have never been inside.

We step into a big front hall. It's dead silent inside. After a few moments, a man appears.

"How may I help you?" He speaks in a hushed voice.

"We need to plan a funeral," I say. "My dad needs some help."

The man steps closer to my father.

"A loved one?" he asks.

"My wife." My dad's voice cracks when he says the words.

"Please come this way," the man says.

He leads us into a paneled office. My dad and I sit down. The man asks questions about "the deceased." After my dad answers, the man starts to ask about the funeral and what my dad wants. He helps my dad put together an announcement for the newspaper. He says he will check with the police to find out when the body will be released, and then they can schedule the funeral. They talk for almost an hour. My dad seems to relax. The man says he can take care of all the details. He tells my dad not to worry.

I take my dad home and make him go upstairs to lie down. He was up all night, and here it is, almost night again.

I was up all night too. But I'm too geared up to sleep.

Instead, I slump in front of the TV and flip through channels. The whole time, my mind replays what happened in front of the garage the night before. The man. Tracie telling my dad to do something. My dad lunging at the man. The gun shots. Tracie falling. More gunshots. The man falling. My dad, standing there, a gun in his hand, looking dazed.

Maybe I didn't like Tracie much, but my dad did. And maybe I've been mad at him since he started seeing her and got even madder when he told me he wanted to marry her. But I'm not mad now. I'm old enough to know that my dad loved Tracie, maybe as much as he loved my mom. Maybe even more. I'm old enough, too, to realize how awful it must be for him, losing two wives. Losing? What am I saying? They weren't lost. They were murdered—by the same man. But why? Why did that man come back? What had he been planning to do? Did he come to our house to kill my dad? What would that have accomplished?

I'm still slouched on the couch the next morning when the phone rings. I don't bother reaching for it. Let it go to voice mail.

My dad comes downstairs about an hour later. His hair is all messed up, and his eyes are red. He doesn't look as if he's slept much.

"Shouldn't you be at school?" he says.

"I didn't feel like it."

He nods. "It's Friday. When I was in school, nothing much ever got done on Friday."

I don't tell him that things are different at my school. We have tests on Fridays. We have a couple scheduled for today. But I don't care about them. I'm too tired to care about anything.

My dad heads for the front door.

"Where are you going, Dad?"

"To the club. To check on things. I'll be back in a couple of hours." He pauses. "The funeral director called this morning. The police are going to release the body tomorrow. We're going to have the funeral on Monday. The funeral home is sending someone over to help pick out some clothes. If she gets here before I do, help her out, okay? I put all of Tracie's favorite dresses on the bed."

I stare at him.

"You don't have to go inside, Finn," my dad says. There's an edge of impatience in his voice, and it makes me feel ashamed. "Just show her where the room is. You think you can do that?"

I nod. "I'm sorry, Dad. It's just—"

He sighs and waves his hand to silence me.

"It's okay, son," he says. "I understand. But do just this one thing for me, okay?"

Eight
LILA

When I told Aunt Jenny that I was going to stay here until the lease was up in seven weeks, it seemed like a good idea. It felt like I was doing the right thing.

Two days after he dies, I'm not so sure anymore.

First, it's harder than I could have imagined to read the newspaper and listen to the news and hear his name. It's even harder when they mention—they always do—that he was out of prison for less than seventy-two hours when, as they put it, he "killed again." But the worst is to hear so-called commentators use my father as an example of how the justice system is broken. Let a killer out of prison, they say, and only a fool would be surprised that he runs true to his colors and murders someone else. Some of them say that anyone who kills should be locked up for life. The same people say that a person who kills twice is an argument for reinstating capital punishment. Turn the other cheek once, and you're a good person. Turn it twice, and you're an idiot. Better to deal with the problem once and for all.

Second, I hate to admit it, but I miss Aunt Jenny. She's never been anything but disapproving of my father, but she has always been loving to me. She raised me as if I were her own child. She pestered me about my homework. She encouraged me to join sports teams, to try out for school plays, to sing in the choir at church, to volunteer at the local seniors' center, to be, as she put it, a member of the community. To be good. And she listened. Okay, so there were some things—things about my father—that I learned never to discuss with her. But if there was anything else on my mind, she stopped what she was doing and she gave me her full attention. She never told me what to do. Instead, she always asked me what I thought was the right thing. And I always figured things out. But she isn't here with me now. And even if she were, I don't think I'd talk to her about my father. I would be too afraid of what she might say. And, depending on the words that came out of her mouth, I'd be afraid that I would hate her. Then I would be alone forever.

Finally, there's the question of the funeral.

It's Saturday afternoon. I've just come back from buying some groceries—a few apples, a container of yogurt, a can of tuna, a box of macaroni and cheese,

some milk, a loaf of bread, some frozen peas and—
I can't stop myself—a newspaper. I've put the food away,
and I have the newspaper spread out on the kitchen
table. I'm paging through it, scanning for any news
about my father.

There's nothing.

But my eye catches sight of a familiar name. *Newsome.*
On the obituary page.

It's a death notice for Tracie Newsome, "beloved
wife of Robert Newsome, loving stepmother to Finn
Newsome." There's a picture of her. She's pretty. *Was*
pretty. The little article doesn't say she was shot to death.
Instead, it says she died "suddenly and tragically in the
prime of life." It mentions her passion for her friends, her
love of an afternoon or evening on the town, her support
for charitable causes.

Someone knocks at the door.

It's the woman detective. Detective Sanders.

"I was on my way home," she says. "So I thought I'd
drop by instead."

Instead of what? I wonder.

"They've released the body," she says. "Your father,
I mean. They want to know where to send him."

I stare at her. Where to send him? What is she
talking about?

She looks at me like she's studying for a test.

"Can I come in for a minute, Lila?" she asks.

I step aside to let her pass. She closes the door gently behind her.

Now that she's inside, I feel I have to offer her something—tea or coffee. But she shakes her head.

"I'm fine," she says. She glances around our—my—bare apartment. "They want to know what funeral home to send the body to," she says in a soft voice. "Have you given any thought to the arrangements?"

I shake my head and feel like an idiot. I have no idea what I thought was going to happen, but, no, I haven't given any thought to the arrangements.

"Lila," she says, "I'm sorry to have to ask this, and I don't mean any offense by it, but do you have any money to pay for a funeral? Did your father have an insurance policy or anything like that?"

"I don't think so," I tell her. Knowing my father, I doubt it.

She pulls a small folded paper from her jacket pocket and holds it out to me. It's a brochure.

"The city has a program," she says. "It pays funeral costs when next of kin can't afford to."

I take the brochure from her, but I don't look at it. Something is wrong with my eyes all of a sudden. They won't focus. I can't read the words.

"I can call them if you want," Detective Sanders says. "Would that be okay?"

I nod.

"Okay." She smiles at me. It makes her look like a regular person instead of a cop. "Okay. I'll get in touch with them first thing in the morning. I'll tell them how to contact you." She glances around again. "How are you holding up? Is everything okay?"

I nod again.

"I can put you in touch with victims' services," she says. "In case you need anything or want to talk to someone."

"I'm fine," I say. As fine as anyone can be whose father just killed someone and then was killed himself.

She pulls something else from her pocket. It's a business card. She writes something on it before she gives it to me.

"It's the phone number for victims' services," she says. "Just in case you need some help with something. My number is on there too. Okay?"

"Okay."

After she leaves, I put the brochure and the business card on the kitchen table. I sit down. I look at the newspaper again. It's still open to the death notice for Tracie Newsome. I read it one more time.

Nine
FINN

John calls me. So does Geordie. They both say they're sorry about Tracie. They're both smart enough and know me well enough not to call her my mom. They ask how my dad is holding up. They ask me if I want company or if I want to go out and do something. I tell them no on both counts, even though the real answer is yes. I'd love to get out and away from here. But I feel like the right thing to do is to stay home with my dad.

Matthew Goodis, who manages Dad's club, drops by on Saturday afternoon. When I answer the door, he says, "Sorry about what happened, Finn. Is your dad home?" He looks over my shoulder as if he expects to see my dad standing there.

"He's upstairs," I say. "Come in. I'll get him for you."

He steps inside. I go to get my dad. He's in his bedroom, sitting on the bed, holding a silver-framed picture of Tracie and him on their wedding day. He isn't crying or anything. He's just staring at it.

"Matthew is here," I tell him.

He stares at the picture for a few seconds longer before setting it on his bedside table and standing up. He looks tired, but he follows me downstairs. Matthew says he's sorry to be a bother but that there are some things about the club that need to be straightened out.

"That's okay," my dad says. He and Matthew go into my dad's home office at the back of the house. They're there for a long time, and neither of them is smiling when they come out. Well, why would they be? My dad is all broken up about Tracie, and Matthew knows it.

"At least that's one less thing to worry about," Matthew says before he leaves the house. "But I sure wish none of this has happened"

"So do I," my dad says.

"What was he talking about?" I ask my dad after Matthew is gone.

"Huh?" my dad says.

"What's one less thing to worry about?"

"Business," he says. "There's an act we've been trying to book. We got it."

My dad goes back upstairs. He doesn't come down for supper. He spends the next day fussing over the funeral arrangements. I hear him call the funeral director at least five or six times.

Before I know it, it's Monday.

* * *

The funeral service is held in the funeral home because neither my dad nor Tracie went to church, not even to get married.

The place is packed, which surprises me at first. Then I think, just because I never liked Tracie, that doesn't mean she didn't have friends. She had plenty of them, women she called her *girl*friends, even though they're all pushing forty. They're all there in little black dresses. They're all like Tracie—perfect hair, perfect makeup and expensive clothes that they hope make them look younger than they really are, and lots of jewelry given to them by their rich husbands. All of Tracie's close friends started out like Tracie. They were all secretaries or flight attendants or cocktail waitresses at fancy bars and clubs, all on the hunt for men with money. They stick together because, unlike my mom, they never quite fit into the social circle they most wanted to be part of—the really rich women who grew up in big houses and went to private schools and Ivy League universities, and who look down on people like Tracie. They look down on my dad too.

Besides Tracie's friends, I see a bunch of people who work at the club and who probably think it's good for their careers to show sympathy for the boss in his time of grief. I see some of Dad's best customers too. Also some neighbors. And my friends—a whole bunch of them. Some are there because they're my buddies, like John and Geordie. Some are there because it means they get to skip school. But they're nice about it. They come up to me after the service while I'm waiting for the funeral home people to put the casket in the hearse so we can all drive to the cemetery. They tell me how sorry they are and how horrible it must be to lose two people like that, first my mother and then my stepmother. Some of my teachers are there too. They shake my hand and tell me they've been thinking of me. They shake my dad's hand and express their sympathy.

All my friends except John and Geordie go back to school after the service. A lot of the people from the club leave too. The rest of us pile into cars to drive to the cemetery. We have a police escort to make sure that all the cars stay together, even when we come to intersections. I ride in the front car with my dad. But as soon as we get to the cemetery, I hang back and wait for John and Geordie. I stick with them when the minister says some more words over the coffin and when the coffin is lowered into the ground. I stay with them until my father breaks down sobbing. Then I go to him and put an arm on his shoulder. I feel like his dad rather than the other way around as I pull him gently away from the grave and tell him that everything is going to be okay.

That's when I look up and see her standing in the distance. She isn't part of the funeral, but she's there anyway—the girl from the police station, the one whose father died. The one I talked to and thought about afterward. Mostly what I thought about was that I must have sounded like some kind of psycho: *I saw two people die. They were shot.* Like that made me special or something.

I wonder what she's doing here and how she even knew there was a funeral. Then I remember that the cops called my father by name. She must have heard about it on the news or read about it in the newspaper. And here she is. But why?

"Finn? Hey, Finn, where are you going?" John calls to me.

I tell him I'll be right back. At least, I think I do.

Ten

LILA

Don't do it, I told myself when I woke up this morning. Don't do what you've been thinking about all night. Don't go.

But here I am. It's like there's a rope attached to me and someone is pulling it, reeling me in, like a fish on a line. Every step of the way, I tell myself it's a bad idea. But that invisible rope keeps tugging me until I find myself standing in the middle of a cemetery in the middle of town. The place is so massive that at first I can't see anything but trees that must have been growing since even before my father was born. It's so big that after I finally find the right place, all I can hear is the murmur of the man who is standing in front of the open hole in the ground, reading from a small book, and the trill of a bird overhead somewhere in one of the trees. There are no traffic sounds. No city sounds.

I watch. There are quite a few people here. I wonder if there were more at the funeral home where the paper said the service was going to be held. Probably. I've been to funerals before, mostly funerals of some of the old people in the church that Aunt Jenny goes to and where I sing in the choir. Aunt Jenny makes me go to the funerals. She says it's the right thing to do. It's a way to honor people. It's a way to let them know that they were important to the community. So I know the way it works. I know that there are lots of people who go to the service for the same reason that Aunt Jenny makes me go, because it's the right thing to do, because it's expected. And I know that fewer people go to the cemetery for the actual burial because, besides the fact that it isn't required, it's scarier. It's hard to see a person lowered into the ground and to watch earth being shoveled over them because you know that wherever their soul may be, their body is in the ground and it will be there forever, in the dark, away from life.

I see Robert Newsome standing closest to the man who is reading the final words. His head is bowed. I see his son too. Finn, according to the newspaper. His head is not bowed. He is looking at his father, not at the ground. Then the man who has been reading stops. He nods at another man standing back from the mourners. That man steps forward, and the coffin begins a slow descent into the grave.

That's when Finn looks at me—right at me.

I step back.

He steps forward.

He is coming toward me. He walks slowly at first, and I hesitate. Then he walks faster, as if he's afraid I will turn and run before he can reach me. And that's exactly what I feel like doing—running. I have no business being here. Not now. Not at *this* funeral.

But I had no choice.

Even when I was sitting on the bus telling myself it was a bad idea, I was thinking, but when would be a better time? How do I even know I will have another chance? According to the newspaper, Finn's dad is well-off. What if Finn goes to a private school? What if he goes to a boarding school far away?

Sure, there's always his dad. But I can't bring myself to talk to him. It doesn't matter what they say, it doesn't matter who did what first or why they did it, the fact remains that his dad killed my dad.

His dad killed my dad.

I think that's why I don't run away. It's why I stand my ground.

Finn gets closer, and I see that he is smiling. Sort of. There's a smile on his face. And a big question mark. He's wearing a black suit and a black tie. His shirt is dove-gray. He looks like a billboard ad in that suit. When he's near enough for me to see that his eyes are blue, he slows down again, the way you do when you're getting close to a small animal and don't want to frighten it. He stops a few feet from me.

"I thought it was you," he says. His smile widens, but just for a second. Then it fades, as if he's unsure of himself and of me. "I was surprised to see you."

"I heard the police say your dad's name," I say. That, at least, is the truth. "Then I heard on TV about what happened." That's also the truth, as far as it goes. "It said in the paper where the funeral was going to be."

If he thinks it's odd that a complete stranger would show up at his stepmother's funeral, he doesn't say so. Instead he says, "Thank you." Then he says, "My name is Finn."

"I know. I saw it in the paper."

He nods. There is a long silence between us, and he looks at me as if he's waiting for something. It takes me forever to figure out what.

"I'm Lila," I say.

"Lila." He seems to enjoy saying my name. "Thanks for coming, Lila."

We stand there looking at each other. I feel like I should say something. But he starts first.

"I thought maybe you thought I was crazy, the way I talked about it at the police station," he says slowly. "You know, telling you I saw people killed and not saying it was my stepmother."

And my father, I think.

"It's just…" His eyes turn watery. "It happened before."

He means his mother.

"I was seven."

So was I, I want to say. You were seven when you lost your first mother. I was seven when I lost my father for the first time.

Someone calls his name, and he turns.

"Just a minute," he yells back. "My dad," he says when he turns to me again. "I guess I have to go."

I need to talk to him. I *have* to talk to him. But I'm paralyzed.

He starts to move and then swings back.

"Can I call you?" he asks. "Or is that too weird?"

It's too weird, I think. It's way too weird. But there I am, nodding again. I start to recite the phone number at the apartment.

"Wait!" He holds up a hand, and I clamp my mouth shut. He digs in his pants pocket and pulls out a cell phone. "Okay," he says.

I say my phone number again, and he punches the number in. He smiles shyly when he's finished. This time when his dad calls him, he swings around. I watch him walk away. He and his dad and their friends go back to a string of cars that are parked along the cemetery road. They get in and drive away.

I check my watch.

I have to get going. Detective Sanders has some forms for me to fill out. She put me in touch with someone. My father's funeral is this afternoon. I want to say something about him, but so far I haven't decided what.

Eleven

FINN

I leave the girl—Lila—behind and join my dad and John and Geordie. We head for the club. People have already gathered in one of the private rooms, and my dad says more will probably drop by. They have come to express their condolences to me and my dad and to talk with him. John and Geordie head straight for the food. They're both into athletics. They're trying to bulk up. When they're not thinking about sports or girls, they're thinking about food.

"Dad, can I take off?" I ask.

"Stay for a while," he says. "People expect it."

I do my best not to make a face.

My dad digs in his pocket and hands me his car keys.

"Stay for half an hour," he says. "Then you can go."

I join John and Geordie. They're stuffing their faces with little sandwiches and cakes.

"This stuff is great," Geordie says through a mouthful of puff pastry. John elbows him. John's mom was my mom's best friend. My mom used to say that John and I have known each other since before we were born. We met Geordie later, in junior high.

"It's a funeral," John hisses at Geordie.

Geordie turns red in the face. John looks at me. Then, just like always when one of us gives Geordie a hard time, we burst out laughing. People stare at us, but we don't care. My dad nods in my direction. I can tell he doesn't mind. If anything, he seems glad that I'm not taking this as hard as I took my mother's death. Well, why would I?

"Come on," I say to my friends. I hold up the car keys. "Let's get out of here."

We go to my place, where I turn Geordie and John loose on the fridge. After Tracie died, people brought over tons of food—casseroles, barbecue chicken, pasta and meatballs, meat pies, fruit pies, cookies, squares. You name it, it's all there in the fridge. They fill their plates.

"You're not eating?" John asks.

"Maybe later," I say.

They eat. We play some video games. They leave before my dad gets home.

The house is quiet.

I head upstairs to get changed. To get to my room, I have to pass my dad's room. His and Tracie's. The door is closed—I never go in there. Why would I? I never liked Tracie. I hated the fact that she was in there with my dad. I hated that she was his wife. It didn't matter how many times he told me that no one could ever replace my mom in his heart. I still hated her.

I guess that's why I stop. Because I'm thinking about Tracie. I'm thinking about how I felt when my dad asked me to show the woman from the funeral home the clothes he had laid out for Tracie to "wear at the funeral." That's the way my dad put it, as if Tracie was a mourner and not the guest of honor.

I did what my dad asked. I showed the woman to the room. I told her my dad had put out things for her to choose from. I showed her the door. But I didn't open it for her. I let her do that for herself. The woman went in. I didn't even look inside. I just waited.

"What about shoes?" she called to me.

Shoes? What about them?

"Your father said he wanted her to look just like she always did. But I don't see any shoes."

At first I thought she was kidding. But she came to the door of the bedroom and looked at me, waiting for an answer.

"Your father made himself very clear to Mr. Stone," she said.

"Mr. Stone?"

"The funeral director."

She *had* to be kidding. What was the guy's first name? Grave? Tomb?

She waited some more.

"In the closet," I said. "The one with the pink stripes on the door."

"Thank you." The woman went back inside the room. I waited until she came out again with one of Tracie's dresses over her arm and a pair of shoes in her hand.

I never went inside. I never offered to help her. And at the funeral, when my dad insisted I pay my last respects, I went up to the coffin. I had no choice. But I didn't look at Tracie. Instead, I looked at the white satin lining of the coffin.

So now when I pass my dad's bedroom, I stop. I reach out and touch the knob. It's cold. I almost pull back. But I refuse to let myself. I grasp the knob and turn it. I push the door open.

The room is a disaster. There are clothes and shoes, scarves and jackets, sweaters and boots everywhere—on the bed, on the loveseat and the two armchairs in the alcove in front of the window, on the floor. Everywhere. They are all Tracie's clothes. The door to Tracie's closet is open. I say closet, but, really, it's more like a room. A small room with shelves and drawers and padded clothes hangers lining three sides of it from the floor right up to the ceiling. Tracie had a lot of clothes. She always took care of them. She put things away as soon as she took them off. I know, because my dad used to tease her about it. Apparently she had a special section for everything—sweaters, slacks, blouses, casual dresses, fancy dresses, scarves, lingerie, sports clothes—and in each section, everything was sorted by color.

I step into the room without noticing what I'm doing. I make my way to the closet, careful not to tread on any of Tracie's things. (Why do I even care?) Then I am standing in the doorway to the closet.

Every clothes hanger is empty. Every shelf is empty. Every drawer has been pulled out and is empty. It's as if someone has broken into the house and ransacked Tracie's closet. What were they looking for? Valuables? A chill runs through me. Nothing else seems out of place in the rest of the house. As far as I can tell—not that I checked or anything—everything seems to be exactly where it should be.

I spin around. I've heard about things like this— thieves aren't stupid. Some of them follow the news and read the obituaries. They check when funerals are going to be held because that's when the family of the dearly departed is guaranteed to be out of the house. When there's no one around, it's a thief's paradise. Which means that whoever was in this room was just getting started. I probably startled them when I got back with John and Geordie.

I freeze. Maybe they're still in the house.

I stand perfectly still and listen.

I hear nothing. Nothing at all.

I step back a pace, meaning to get the phone by the bedside table and call the police.

A thought hits me: what is my dad going to think? He's already shell-shocked. He's already handled too much. He could have been killed himself. Tracie *was* killed. I slump against the door to the closet. Maybe I hated Tracie, but my dad was in love with her. Then, out of the blue, that man showed up and my dad had to watch Tracie die, up close. He had to watch someone murder her. The same man who murdered my mom. My stomach clenches, like someone has grabbed it and is wrenching it to make a point: Think about your dad, stupid. Think about how he must feel. Think about how you would feel if someone you loved was killed right in front of you. Think about how he's going to feel when he sees this.

That's when the dam breaks, and the tears start to flow—for the first time since Tracie died, I cry. But I do it for my dad, and I do it out of shame. I don't do it for her.

Twelve
LILA

My father's funeral isn't anything like Mrs. Tracie Newsome's funeral. The only thing it has in common is that it's held in a funeral home. It's not a bad-looking place either. But as far as I can tell, it's in the smallest room. I can't blame whoever made that decision. After all, it's the city that's paying for it, not the family. In other words, not me.

My father is in a coffin at the front of the small room by the time I get there. It's not a shiny fancy coffin with brass fittings or whatever, like Mrs. Tracie Newsome's. It's wooden. It's polished. But, if you ask me, it looks like plywood. Pine, maybe, stained to look like something darker and more expensive. Not that it matters. My father is going to be cremated, not buried. The coffin is just for show.

There are several rows of chairs set out in the room facing the coffin. There is a man sitting in the front row. He stands up when I come into the room and smiles when he sees me.

"You must be Lila," he says.

I nod.

"I'm Peter Struthers. I knew your dad when he was in prison. Maybe he mentioned me?"

I shake my head. I've never heard the name Peter Struthers before.

"I heard about what happened. I wanted to drop by to pay my respects."

I don't know what to say. I don't want to think about my dad in prison. Ever since he died, I've been working at trying to remember him before that, when he was still my dad.

Maybe Peter Sruthers reads my mind, because all of a sudden he looks ill at ease.

"I just wanted to drop by for a minute," he said. "I didn't mean to intrude."

It sounds like he's getting ready to leave. Good.

"Anyway…" He shuffles back and forth and then sticks a hand into his pocket. "I wrote down my phone number," he says. "I know you and your dad haven't had much time together. I got to know him pretty well. If you ever want to talk about him, or if there's anything I can do, please feel free to call me. I mean it." He hands me a neatly folded piece of paper.

I take it, but I don't look at it. "Well," he says finally, "I should get going. I wish we could have met under happier circumstances."

Sure, I think. Like I'm even remotely interested in getting to know an ex-con.

He leaves, and I'm glad. I sit down in the chair next to the one he was in. For the longest time, I am the only person in the room. Then I hear a rustle behind me, and I turn around and see Detective Sanders. She stands at the door looking around. When she sees me, she starts toward me.

"How are you holding up, Lila?" she asks.

I tell her I'm fine.

She sits down beside me.

"It's tough when you've been away as long as your father was," she says, as if he's been out of the country and has simply lost touch with all his old buddies instead of having spent ten years at state expense after guaranteeing that no decent person would ever want to have anything to do with him ever again. Except me, of course.

A man from the funeral home comes through a door at the front of the room. He glances around. If he's surprised to see so few mourners, he manages to hide it. He comes over to me and, in a hushed voice, asks if I'd like to begin or if I'd like to wait a few more minutes.

"You can begin," I say.

I know it won't take long. The man told me the service he was going to say. He asked me if it was okay. I asked him to make it short.

He starts reading something sappy about death and dying. Even though I promised myself I wouldn't, I start crying. Detective Sanders pulls out a small packet of tissues and hands it to me. I wipe my eyes.

The man finishes reading and asks me if I want to say anything. I shake my head. And that's it. That's all there is.

My father is to be cremated. I have a little card that tells me when I can pick up his ashes. I still haven't decided what I am going to do with them.

Two more men appear and wheel the coffin out of the room. I stand up. So does Detective Sanders.

"What did you want to ask me?" I say.

She frowns. "Ask you? Nothing."

"But I thought—" My cheeks turn red when I realize my mistake. "I'm sorry," I say.

"It's okay. You need a lift home?"

I want to say no, but she's been nice enough to come.

We walk out to her car and get in. She pulls out from her parking spot at the curb.

"So," I ask after a few blocks, "is there anything new?"

She glances away from the road for a moment.

"It looks pretty open-and-shut," she says. "When it's all over, if you want, you can request a copy of the police report."

"Do you know why he did it?" I want to add, *And if you do, would you tell me?*

She hesitates.

"Did your dad need money, Lila?"

"What do you mean?"

"He just got out of prison. I know he came out with a little money. And he had a job, correct? But he only worked for a couple of days. He hadn't gotten paid yet."

I nod.

"He paid the rent on your place, first and last. That must have taken most of what he had."

"It did."

She glances at me again.

"How did he cover day-to-day expenses?"

"I've had a job since I was thirteen." First delivering flyers. Then working checkout at a grocery store. Then as shift manager at a video store. I put in a lot of hours. I needed the money to pay for bus fare to go and see him regularly. Then I decided to save up for when he got out. "We were going to use my savings until he got paid. And I was going to look for a job."

"What about school?"

"What about it?"

"I spoke to your Aunt Jenny."

The flare in my eyes is automatic. I can't help it. I hear Aunt Jenny's name, and right away I think of all the things she must have told Detective Sanders about my father.

Detective Sanders reads the look on my face.

"It's my job, Lila," she says.

"What did she say?"

"That you loved your dad. That you went to see him regularly. That you spent all your time either working or studying. That you wanted to make your father proud of you by going to university." We're close to the house now. She pulls over to the curb. "She said you were hoping to get a scholarship but that it didn't work out."

I'm imagining Aunt Jenny and her disapproving face.

"Did she tell you that if I'd spent fewer weekends going to see my father and less time working, I'd probably have got that scholarship?" She sure told me often enough.

"No, she didn't." She turns and looks out the front window of the car for a few moments. "Did you tell you dad about it? About not getting a scholarship?"

I'm not sure what she's getting at, but I am sure that if she tells me, I won't like it. I shake my head.

"Did you know that your Aunt Jenny told him?"

My head whips around to stare at her. "*What?* When did my dad talk to Aunt Jenny? Or did she call him? That's it, isn't it? She hates him. She always did. She called him, didn't she? She called him and told him so he'd feel bad. She wanted him to send me home, is that it?"

Detective Sanders doesn't say anything for another few moments. She just looks at me. Her face is unreadable. It's her professional face, I think. It's her on-the-job face. Her stillness is the same thing. They're both part of what she does every day when she talks to people. She studies them. Maybe she even knows some tricks about how to read them. You have to know that when you're a cop, especially when you're a detective. You have to know how to watch people, how to look for the tics and twitches that give them away, how to have some idea when they're lying to you and when they're telling the truth. You learn how to make silence work for you too. How to leave things hanging long enough that it makes the other person uncomfortable and that person starts talking. With suspects and people with something to hide, that's a big plus. The more they talk, the better the chances are that they'll say something that will give them away.

"She says he called her, Lila. She was surprised. He wanted her to talk you into going home."

"And she decided to tell him I didn't get a scholarship?"

Detective Sanders nods—and waits.

"Oh," I say. I remember her asking me if my dad needed money. I couldn't figure out why she'd asked, but I get it now. "You think that's what it was all about? You think that's why he went over to the Newsomes? You think he wanted money for me so I could go to university?"

She doesn't answer. Instead, she does what she does best. She asks another question.

"Did he say anything to you about Mr. Newsome?"

I shake my head.

"Did he mention anything to you about money?"

"You asked me that before. The answer is still no."

"School?"

"No."

She sighs and leans back again the car seat.

"You should call your aunt, Lila," she says. "You're a smart girl. You're young. Your whole life is ahead of you. You should go home. You should go to school. I know you love your dad. You can still make him proud."

I know she means well. At least, I'd like to think she does. I'd like to think she came to the funeral because she cares, not just because she wanted to pump me for information. But I don't know for sure. After all, she's a cop.

"Thanks for the lift," I say as I open the car door.

"Do you still have my card?"

I nod.

"Call me," she says. "Anytime. For anything. I mean it, Lila. Even if you just want to talk."

I nod again. She may be a cop, but she seems okay.

Thirteen
FINN

So there I am, leaning against the door to Tracie's closet, staring at the mess inside and crying like a baby. It's like once I've started, I can't stop. I'm glad John and Geordie aren't there. They know exactly how I feel about Tracie. If they'd seen me like this, they would have been sure I was ready for the loony bin.

I hear something behind me—a little rush of air.

"Finn, what are you doing?"

I spin around, and there's my dad. He's in the doorway to his room, a look of surprise on his face. I can't tell what put it there. Maybe it's the tears, or maybe it's the fact that I'm in his room. Or—I glance around at all the clothes on the floor—maybe he thinks I'm the one who trashed the place.

"Dad, I—"

"What's going on?"

"It wasn't me."

"What?"

"All this stuff." I sweep my hands around the room. "It wasn't me."

"I know."

"We should call the cops. We should check the rest of the house."

My dad comes into the room. "It's okay, Finn. It's not what you think."

"But someone was here, Dad. Someone did this." I cross the room and reach for the phone. My dad comes toward me. He takes the phone from my hand.

"It's okay, Finn. We weren't broken into. It was me."

I hear him say it, but I don't register the meaning of the words.

"It was me, Finn." He hangs his head. "I don't know what came over me. Rage, I guess. That's what it felt like. I was in here—in there." He nods toward the bed. "I could smell her perfume on the pillow. And I thought about what he said—and what I said. I should have handled it differently. I should have—" He broke off. It took a minute for him to gather himself. "I just went crazy, I guess."

What he said?

"Who do you mean, Dad?"

He sinks down on the bed.

"Dad?"

"Louis Ouimette. The man who killed Tracie. And your mother."

"What did he say to you?"

"He called me."

"He *called* you?" That is news to me. I sit on the bed beside my father.

"The day before he showed up here. He called me and left a message on my voice mail. I shouldn't have erased it. But what was I supposed to think? I mean, how dare he call me and make demands like that, after what I did for him. How *dare* he?"

"What do you mean? What did you do for him, Dad?"

My dad shakes his head slowly.

"You don't remember him, Finn?"

I'm drawing a blank. I feel like something important is happening here, but it's passing me right by.

"You were just a kid," my dad says finally. "You were hit pretty hard by what happened. You probably blocked it out. That child psychologist I took you to said that would happen. You remember the psychologist, right, Finn? I took you to see him after Mom died?"

I remember. He was a tall man with round glasses who smelled like pipe tobacco. I went to see him every week for over a year.

"Ouimette used to work at the club," my dad says.

"What are you talking about, Dad? What club?"

"My club. The Siren."

"He worked there?" I can't seem to get a grip on the idea. "Mom's killer worked there?"

My dad nods, and I feel like an idiot. It happened ten years ago, and here I am, being surprised by an important fact. Why didn't I know this already? Why hadn't I asked a million questions about what happened instead of sticking my fingers in my ears and squeezing my eyes shut, as if I could make it all go away? What kind of son am I that I didn't want to know more—that I didn't want to know everything?

"I knew what he was before Matthew hired him," my dad says. "I knew he was an ex-con. But I believed what I was told. I believed he was clean. And he was honest about his record. He didn't try to hide it. I guess I was dumb enough to think that counted for something. I thought that if he was up-front about his past, about all the arrests and the drugs, if he could tell the truth about that, then he must be telling the truth when he said it was all behind him. So I decided to give him a chance. I okayed Matthew's decision, Finn, and there isn't a single day that I don't think about how things would have been different if I hadn't."

I wanted to shake him. I wanted to scream at him, *What were you thinking?* He's probably right—if he hadn't okayed that stupid decision, my mom would still be alive. So would Tracie, except that she never would have been part of my life. My dad would never have even looked at her. Why would he, when my mom was still around?

"What did he say when he called you, Dad?"

"He wanted money."

What?

"Can you believe it?" my dad said. "He gets out of prison after—after what he did. And he calls me and tells me he wants money."

"Did you call him back?"

My dad looks at me like I'm crazy.

"Of course not! Why would I do that? I didn't owe him a thing. He owed me. He killed my wife!"

"Did you call the police?"

"I didn't call anyone." He's angry, but I can't tell if he's angry with me or with himself. "I just deleted the call and went on with my life. I didn't think he'd have the nerve to show up at my house, not after what he'd done."

"Is that why he was here? For money?"

My dad nods.

"I told him no. That's when he shot Tracie."

"I don't get it, Dad. Why would he ask you for money? He must have known you wouldn't give it to him."

"So you'd think," my dad says. "He must have been on something. There are more drugs in prison than there are on the streets. There's something wrong with the way they run those places, if you ask me. Some guys go in there straight and come out addicts. If only I'd never heard of him."

Yeah. If only.

"You want me to help you clean up all this stuff, Dad?"

He shakes his head. "I'll deal with it. It's got to go anyway. Maybe someone else can make good use of it."

I stare at all the dresses and skirts and sweaters, the blouses and scarves, the shoes and sandals, the lingerie. It's right out there where I can see it, not that I want to.

"You want me to get you some boxes?"

"It's okay, Finn," my dad says. "I'll take care of it. It's my mess."

He's still sitting on the bed when I leave the room to go downstairs. When I come up again a few hours later and glance through the open door, he's still there. He hasn't moved.

Fourteen
LILA

After Detective Sanders drops me off, I go inside and put the kettle on to make myself a cup of tea. It's what Aunt Jenny and I used to do every day after I got home from school. She'd put the kettle on, and we'd have a cup of tea while she asked me about school. Then I'd get out my books and we'd sit at the kitchen table together, both of us doing homework. Aunt Jenny is a nurse. For most of the time I lived with her, she worked the overnight shift so that she could go to school during the day. She was always upgrading her skills, always improving herself. It was nice, just the two of us, our books and notes spread out all over the kitchen table, studying. While I wait for the kettle to boil, I wonder if Detective Sanders is right. Maybe I should just go home. I miss Aunt Jenny, and I know she misses me.

But how can I leave now? I went to see my dad regularly for years. It was always just him and me. When I was little and Aunt Jenny used to have to take me, she never came inside with me. She told me, "You probably want time alone with your dad." But I know now that that wasn't the real reason she didn't come with me. I know now that she didn't like my father. Worse, she didn't respect him. To her, he was weak. It was the only reason she could think of that he didn't take himself in hand, as she put it, that he didn't shake off his demons, that he constantly disappointed my mother before finally catching her in his own vortex of misery and weakness. It was the reason he didn't see what he was doing or where she was heading.

Maybe Aunt Jenny was right at one time. But gradually over all those years I went to see him, I saw a different father from the one I remembered when I was little.

He smiled when he saw me.

He asked me about school.

He asked me to tell him what I had learned, and he listened intently to my answers.

He was in the here and now. He was clean on the outside—scrubbed and combed and shaven—as well as on the inside. I saw light in his eyes instead of shadows. I saw interest instead of oblivion. He talked about the long-term future instead of the next drink or the next fix.

He was different.

He was good.

So what happened? How is it that a man—my father—who spoke for a whole year about what he wanted to do when he got out, went and killed a woman? He said he wanted to find a place where we could live together. ("But only if you want to, Lila. You don't have to. You know that, right? If you want to stay with your Aunt Jenny, that's okay.") He said he wanted to learn to cook. ("So I can make a meal for you. I remember all those eggs you used to make for me. You were just a little girl. But you knew about eggs and protein.") He said he wanted to get a library card. ("They have a library in here. At first I thought it was stupid—big books with big words written years ago by guys who were dead before I was born. But you know what? Once you get into one of those things, it's not so bad.") He talked about getting a decent job. ("Sure, I know I'm going to have to start with scut work. What else are you going to do when you're a con? But they have programs, Lila. They say you can change, if you want it bad enough. You can do anything if you want it bad enough.")

It's true. You *can* do anything...

...if you want it bad enough.

What I want: to understand how a man who talked so much about a future that was different from his past could, three days after he got out of prison, take a gun to another man's house and kill that man's wife and then try to kill that man.

That's what I want. And I want it bad. I guess that's why I go out even though it's dark already. I ask a bus driver for directions. Half an hour later, I'm standing in what's called the entertainment district. Competing bass lines throb out of clubs and rock the night. People are out on the streets in front of bright signs. They are talking and smoking. The women—most of them look like girls—wear short tight dresses and impossibly high heels. They wear glittery makeup and dangly jewelry. The guys are dressed in sharp suits, their hair gelled and spiked. Everyone eyes everyone else. Everyone is on the make.

I scan the neon signs until I find the one I'm looking for. *The Siren.* Robert Newsome's club.

There's a line outside—made-up girls and gelled-up guys waiting to get in. At the head of the line, blocking the door, stands a massive man, his arms crossed over his chest. I approach him.

He looks down at me—at my jeans, at my jean jacket, at my clean-scrubbed face.

"We got a dress code, sugar," he says.

"I don't want to get in. My dad used to work here."

It's like talking to a block of granite. There's no expression on his face. I get no response.

"He worked here ten years ago," I say.

"Ten years ago, I was in junior high."

He isn't even looking at me.

"They say he shot Mr. Newsome's wife," I say.

Mr. Granite looks down at me again.

"You're being a nuisance, sugar," he says. "You know what I do when someone is a nuisance?" He turns and nods to a slightly smaller version of himself, who starts toward us.

"I mean it," I say. "My dad was in prison for it. They say he shot Mrs. Newsome. Ten years ago."

The junior version of Mr. Granite perks up.

"I heard about that. That junkie guy, what's his name?"

"Louis Ouimette," I say.

He nods. "That's it. That's the guy." He looks triumphantly at Mr. Granite. "Same guy who just killed Tracie and tried to kill Mr. Newsome," he says. "But Mr. Newsome plugged him first. How could you not know about that, man? It just happened. They just had the funeral. You didn't go?"

Mr. Granite shakes his head: *Of course I didn't go.* When Junior looks at him like he's the biggest loser in the world, he says, "What? You did?"

"The man's wife was shot dead right in front of him," Junior says. "Yeah, I went."

I decide he might be more helpful than Mr. Granite. When I talk next, I direct myself to him.

"I'm trying to find someone who worked here back when the first Mrs. Newsome got shot," I say. "Anyone."

Junior eyes me closely. "I know you," he says. "You were there too. At the funeral." He looks at Mr. Granite again, as if to underline once more the fact that attending the funeral was the right thing to do.

"Is there anyone I can talk to?" I ask again.

"There's Mr. Newsome," Junior Granite says. "And Mr. Goodis."

"Who's Mr. Goodis?" I ask.

"The manager."

Great. There's no way I want to talk to Mr. Newsome. And I'm betting Mr. Goodis won't be much better. If he's management, he's probably close to Mr. Newsome.

"Nobody else was around back then?"

Junior Granite looks me up and down.

"Well," he says, "there's Dodo."

"Dodo?"

"He used to be a bouncer. Had an accident a couple of years back. Mr. Newsome gave him a different job. He's the janitor now."

"Is he here?"

"Dodo? He's always here," Mr. Granite says. He's grinning, like he's about to sit down on a whoopee cushion and he knows it and relishes the rude noise that's about to cut the air.

"That was really your dad who killed Tracie?" Junior Granite says.

I nod.

"C'mon." He waves me away from Mr. Granite.

"You're not supposed to leave your post," Mr. Granite rumbles at him.

"I'll remember that next time you need to step away from the line for a minute or two," Junior Granite shoots back. He leads me to the side of the building and starts down the long dark alley that runs between it and the building next door.

I stop at the mouth of the alley. Junior Granite glances back over his shoulder.

"You want to see Dodo or not?" he says. "He's in the back."

Alarm bells sound in my head. How many times has Aunt Jenny told me never to go off with strangers? How many times has she told never to venture into a dark alley? Yet here I am about to do both.

Junior Granite stops a few paces into the alley. He turns back to look at me.

"Your choice," he says with a shrug.

I peer into the alley and don't see any light at the end of it. But he's right, it is my choice.

"How come you call him Mr. Newsome but you call her Tracie?" I ask.

Even in the gloom of the alley, I see the white of his teeth.

"She was always telling people to call her that. Mr. N., he didn't like it. But Tracie...she was friendly." There's a note of disdain in his voice, as if he didn't respect her for that.

I start after him.

He doesn't wait for me to catch up but instead keeps walking and disappears from sight before I'm halfway down the alley. When I finally come out the other end, he's standing a few paces away from me, near some concrete steps that lead to the basement of the club. He waits until he sees me before he goes down the steps and pushes open the door. I wait up above.

"Dodo! Hey, Dodo, you there?"

Nothing happens.

Junior Granite turns and looks up at me, his shoulders rolling upward, as if he's about to tell me, *I tried.*

I see a faint light at the bottom of the steps. It gets brighter. A face appears. An old face, black and weathered. A sinewy old man steps out of the basement, a push broom in his hands, and I try hard not to stare. One side of his head is caved in, like a too-soft soccer ball kicked too hard.

"Someone wants to talk to you," Junior Granite says.

Dodo squints at me.

"Her dad used to work here. That guy who shot Mrs. Newsome. Loo-is."

"Lou-*ee*," Dodo says, pronouncing my father's name correctly as he stares at me with new interest. "You Louis's little girl?"

I nod.

Dodo comes up the steps, and I see from the roll of his gait that he's limping. I see too that his left leg is stiff.

"How is your dad?" he asks.

"Dead," Junior Granite said. "You didn't hear? He killed Tracie. Took a shot at Mr. Newsome. And got himself killed."

Dodo doesn't seem surprised by this. I take that as a bad sign.

"I never was much for keeping up with the news," he says. "It's never anything good. Always something bad." He squints at me again. "He used to tell me his little girl looked exactly like his late wife. Your mama must have been a real beauty."

I blush despite myself and am glad for the darkness that hides it.

We hear a roar: "Antoine!"

Dodo looks at Junior Granite.

Junior Granite disappears back into the alley.

Dodo leans on his push broom.

"When did it happen?" he asks me. "Your daddy getting killed, I mean?"

"A couple of nights ago."

"I didn't even know he was out," the old man says. He stands there staring off into space. I'm the one who finally breaks the silence.

"Did you know him well?" I ask.

"We worked together. We both had our troubles. His landed him in the lockup. Mine got me in the hospital and then this damn thing." He balls one hand into a fist and strikes his stiff leg. The *thunk* of knuckle against something equally hard tells me that he has an artificial leg.

"I was wondering…do you know anything about what happened that night, the night the first Mrs. Newsome was shot?"

He stares at me, shaking his head slowly.

"My own daddy was a son of a bitch, if you'll excuse me for saying so," he says. "But he did give me one piece of good advice. Don't ask the question unless you're sure you want the answer."

"With all due respect, Mr. Dodo," I say. "My dad was an alcoholic and a drug addict. He spent ten years in prison. And he just got shot to death. There's nothing you can tell me about him that can upset me or hurt me or shock me." I meant it too, when I said it.

Dodo draws himself up straight.

"You think, huh?" he says. "How about this? Your daddy spent ten years in prison for something he never did."

Fifteen
FINN

When I go downstairs the next morning, my dad's on the phone.

"I see," he says, nodding. He smiles at me when I step into the kitchen. He's shaved and showered. I can smell the aftershave and the soap on him. And the shampoo. He's dressed for success in one of his power suits that he gets tailor-made. He looks like his old self.

"Yes. Okay," he says into the phone. He listens intently before finally saying, "All right. Well, thank you." He hangs up the phone and turns to me. "Sleep well?"

"Okay, I guess." The truth: I tossed and turned all night. I kept thinking about Tracie and replaying the sound of those gunshots and the sight of her falling to the ground. Don't ask me why, but I can't stop wondering if she died as soon as the bullet hit her or

81

if there was some time, even a couple of seconds, when she realized what had happened, when she knew what was going to happen. And it bothers me. It also bothers me that just before it happened, when I heard her voice, I thought, God, why doesn't she shut up once and for all? Then, *blam*, that's exactly what happened. I know my thinking it didn't cause it to happen, but I feel bad about it all the same.

My dad pours himself a refill from the coffee maker on the kitchen counter. I reach for a mug too. I don't drink a lot of coffee, but every so often I need some to get me going in the morning. Today is one of those days.

"That was the police," my dad says, stepping aside to let me at the coffee maker.

"Is everything okay?"

He gives me a peculiar look. "Sure. Why wouldn't it be? They just called to tell me they're filing their final report. Tracie is a homicide. Ouimette was self-defense. It's over, son. Now we have to find a way to move on. You hungry? You want me to make you some eggs?"

"It's okay. I can do it myself."

"Nonsense."

He sets down his mug and starts to take stuff out of the fridge—eggs, milk, butter, cheese, green onions and a loaf of bread. I watch in astonishment as he ties on a chef's apron and starts to whip up a six-egg cheese omelet.

"Dad, I'm not *that* hungry."

He grins at me. "Who says it's all for you?"

He slides four pieces of whole-wheat bread into the toaster oven and turns it on. A few minutes later we're sitting across from each other at the kitchen table scarfing down a terrific omelet. My dad eats like a man who has been starving. He washes down the last mouthful with the rest of his coffee, stands up and starts setting plates into the sink.

"I'll do that, Dad."

"Don't you have to get to school?"

"It's early. I can handle it."

My dad doesn't argue with me.

"I have to get to the club. We're supposed to open the new floor this weekend. I have to check on the details. See you later, okay?"

I sit at the table drinking my coffee even after he's gone. The clock on the wall reads *8:00 AM*. If I'm going to get to school on time, I have to get a move on.

But I stay right where I am.

About the time the late bell is ringing halfway across town, where my school is, I get up and carry my breakfast dishes to the sink. I rinse them and my dad's dishes and set them into the dishwasher.

My phone rings. I check the call display..

John.

"Hey, man, where are you?"

"I'm taking a sick day," I tell him.

"You okay?" There's genuine concern in his voice. "Is everything okay with Rob?"

My dad is famous for telling everyone, even my friends, to call him Rob. So they do.

"Yeah. They closed the case. He's at the club. I just need another day."

"Catch you later?"

"Yeah. Sure. I'll call you."

I leave my phone on the table and head up the stairs to my room. My plan: crawl back into bed, pull the covers up over my head, and try to get the sleep I didn't get last night.

Only I don't make it to my room right away. Instead, I stop at my dad's bedroom. The door is closed—Tracie always insisted on it, like she was afraid I was going to go pawing through her stuff. I guess it never occurred to her that that was pretty much the last thing I would ever do, that I could barely stomach the idea of her and my dad together in the same bed, and the thought of her in that room made me physically ill. But now I push open the door. I don't even know why. I guess to see if my dad did anything about the mess.

The bed is neatly made. There are no clothes on it. There are no clothes on the floor or on the any of the furniture. He must have cleaned up after I went to bed.

I go into the room and cross to Tracie's closet. I open the closet door.

Oh.

It's almost funny, like the kind of thing I used to do when I was a kid and my mom used to tell me to clean up my room. I'd shove everything under my bed, wait half an hour and then invite her to come and take a look. I don't know why I bothered. It never worked.

"Where did you get the idea that shoving things out of the sight is the same thing as tidying up?" she always said.

Now I know.

My poor dad. He probably just wanted to get everything out of sight.

I sigh. I start to close the closet door. Then I decide to do something nice for a change.

I go back down to the kitchen. I take a box of green garbage bags and a roll of masking tape. I dig around in a drawer and find a felt pen. I go back upstairs and I start to fold and sort.

I put all the long-sleeved sweaters in one bag and label it *long-sleeved sweaters*. I put all the blouses in another bag and label it *blouses*. I work my way through slacks, jeans, workout clothes, T-shirts, blazers, scarves, every category of clothing you can think of. I keep everything separate and label everything neatly so that my dad knows what's what and can make decisions about what to do with it. Finally the only things left are…underwear stuff. I don't even want to touch the things. They're all tiny and lacy, and call me a pig, but I can't help thinking what I'm thinking. I scoop everything, all of it, into a bag, seal it and set it aside without labeling it. Out of sight…

I take all the bags out into the hall and set them in a row where my dad won't be able to miss them.

Then I go back to close the closet door. In fact, that's just what I'm doing when I see something hanging out of one of the drawers that line the bottom half of one wall. I pull the drawer open. Jeez, more underwear. I go back out into the hall, unknot the underwear bag, bring it back and scoop the things into it. Before I reseal it, I start to go through all the drawers. Might as well make sure I got everything.

I pull open drawer after drawer.

Empty.

Empty.

Empty.

Empty.

More underwear. Thongs, mostly. She could have opened a lingerie store with all the stuff she had.

Empty.

Empty, and kind of stuck. I slide this particular drawer back and forth a few times. Yeah, definitely stuck. Maybe warped. I try to pull it open again, and this time it sticks for good. I can't open it all the way, and I can't close it.

I get down on my hands and knees. Something is definitely blocking it.

So I pull out the drawer under it. I pull it right out of its frame. Then I reach under the stuck drawer to see if I can figure out what's blocking it.

It's some kind of paper. It probably slipped out and got wedged in there. I pull at it, but it doesn't come out.

It takes a moment to work it free. Finally, I have it. It's an envelope, all crunched at one corner thanks to the drawer opening and closing on it until it jammed.

I toss it aside and go through the rest of the drawers. When I'm satisfied I've emptied everything, I retie the lingerie bag and put it back in the hall. Then I pick up the envelope, close the closet drawer and head to my room. I'm about to throw the envelope on my dresser when I get curious. What if Tracie was hiding it? What if there's something in there she didn't want people to see—like… Hey, maybe the envelope contains incriminating photos of Tracie in some of her tiny, lacy lingerie.

For a minute, I can't decide if that's a reason to open the envelope or a reason to burn it. I mean, do I really want to see…?

I unseal the envelope and pull out what's inside. It's a piece of paper. It doesn't feel like photographic paper, but still, I only peek at it through one half-closed eye.

I'm relieved.

And, I admit it, disappointed.

It isn't a photo of Tracie.

It isn't a photo at all.

It's some kind of bill from what looks like a handyman. Then I remember how my dad is as bad as me when it comes to his things. He's always shoving stuff into drawers and then forgetting where he put them. He's better at the club. At least, he says he is. But he spends a lot of time at home looking for stuff that he's put somewhere but can't remember where. My mom used to tell him that if he added up all the time he spent looking for stuff, it would be years of his life, and that he could have spent those years doing something fun if only he'd been more organized.

I toss the envelope onto my dresser. I'll give it to him later.

I crawl into bed.

* * *

The next thing I know, I'm being blinded by the after-noon sun. I check my clock. It's nearly three. School will be out soon. I reach for my phone. It isn't there.

Right. I left it in the kitchen.

I roll out of bed and go downstairs to retrieve it. When I hit the button for my list of saved numbers, I see hers right under John's. Lila. The girl from the funeral. It was nice of her to show up, especially considering what she told me about her dad.

I don't even hesitate. I call her.

The phone rings twice, three times, four times at the other end. I hear a breathless voice.

"Hello?"

"Lila?"

"Yes?" She sounds guarded, as if she's expecting bad news and is bracing herself.

"It's Finn. From the police station. And the funeral. You gave me your number, remember?"

The pause that follows is so long that there can only be two possibilities—she doesn't remember, or she's trying to figure out what to say to make me go away.

"I remember," she says at last. If there's any way she could sound less enthusiastic, I can't come up with it. I remind myself that her father died. That was why she was at the police station.

"So...how are you doing?"

"I'm kind of busy," she says.

"If there's a better time..."

"No." She doesn't hesitate, not even for a split second. "No. It was a mistake to give you my number. I'm sorry."

I hear the click, but I can't quite believe it. No one has ever hung up on me before. I stand there like an idiot and stare at my phone. Grief, I can understand. But what did she mean when she said, *It was a mistake to give you my number*? Is it just that she isn't interested in talking to anyone, especially a stranger? I can understand that. But that isn't what it sounded like.

Whatever.

I call John. We agree to meet up near school.

* * *

I wait for John about a block from school where none of my teachers will see me, even though I know that none of them would dare challenge my absence today. Last year, the mother of a kid in my class died in a car accident.

He was out for nearly two months with a complete mental breakdown. Well, I can top that. I saw a shooting—two people killed right in front of my eyes, and my father nearly killed. Still, I don't want any hassles. And I sure don't want any awkward moments of forced or even sincere sympathy.

John's hungry. What else is new? So we head to a burger place, where he orders a cheeseburger with bacon, fries with gravy, and a chocolate milkshake.

I order a Coke.

"That's it?" he says.

I shrug, and he nods.

"You okay?" he says.

I tell him, yeah. And then I start to tell him about the girl.

"The one you were talking to at the funeral?" he says. "She's hot. Who is she?"

I explain the little I know about her.

"But you got her number, right?"

"I called her today."

John grins. "And?"

"She hung up on me."

He sits back in his chair, a look of mock astonishment on his face.

"Blown off? By a hot chick? How did *that* happen?" He laughs and drags a couple of French fries through thick gravy before shoving them into his mouth.

"She said she made a mistake when she gave me her number," I say.

"I could have warned her." He chuckles. "So, you're going to call her again, right?"

"Didn't you hear what I just said? She blew me off."

"Yeah, but you've got to ask yourself—if she's not interested, what was she doing at the funeral? Who shows up at the funeral of a complete stranger? I'll tell you who—no one. Unless that person has already met one of the grieving family members—which you said she did, at the police station—and feels for that person, which I bet she does, because you said it yourself, she was there because her father died. Obviously he didn't just drop dead of a heart attack. You don't go to the police station for that. So it must have been something pretty bad. Maybe some grisly car accident. Maybe a hit-and-run. She's obviously grieving, Finn. And she obviously sees you as some kind of kindred soul. That's why she was at the funeral. If I were you—"

I'm not listening to him. Instead, I'm thinking about the girl. She had a reason for being at Tracie's funeral. I'm not sure what it is. I'd like to believe it was me, but maybe it wasn't. No matter what that reason is, John's right about what she must be going through. Her father died. And the fact that she was at the police station means it was something as traumatic as what I saw in my own yard. Maybe she came because she wanted to reach out to someone she thought might understand. And maybe she backed off because she's shy, or she's having a hard time, or whatever.

"What if she hangs up on me again?"

John crosses his arms over his chest. "Are you a man or what?"

I think about that. "Maybe I'll try her again."

"No time like the present, my friend."

"I'll do it later."

"Man up, Finn. Strike while the iron is hot. He who hesitates is lost. *Carpe diem. Tempus*—"

"All right. Jeez." I dig my phone out of my pocket, find her number, hit the right button.

The phone rings at the other end.

No answer.

No voice mail either, so I can't even leave a message.

"Maybe you should drop by her place."

"I don't know where she lives."

"You're pathetic, you know that?" He puts his fork down and digs his own phone out of his pocket. "What's her number?" he says. I tell him. He fiddles around with his phone. I can't see what he's doing. Then: "Murrich," he says. "She lives on Murrich. 1833."

"How do you—?"

He turns his phone around, and I see the screen. He's been on the Internet, doing a reverse number lookup.

"Ball's in your court, dude," he says.

Sixteen
LILA

I wake up the next morning feeling like all I want to do is sleep forever, mainly because I barely slept the night before. "Be careful what you wish for," Aunt Jenny always says. What she means is, what you think you want doesn't always turn out to be the thing you hope it's going to be.

Like going to The Siren the night before and finding someone who knew my father way back when. Hearing Dodo say, "How about this? Your daddy spent ten years in prison for something he never did."

I lie in bed, my covers up over my head. I remember the feeling when I heard him say those words. I remember my whole body being jarred, as if my heart slammed to a stop. I could barely speak.

"What do you mean?" I ask Dodo. I realize I'm holding my breath. I'm going to hear what I've ached to hear practically all my life.

He looks me up and down.

"You seem like a nice girl," he says. "You go to school?"

I nod.

"That's the best thing a young person can do—go to school. That way, maybe you don't end up with a broom in your hand."

"What do you mean?" I ask him again. "About my father? Are you saying he didn't do it?"

He peers at me again, as if weighing the damage his words will do.

"Your daddy," he says carefully, "he had his demons."

"I know. I know all about that."

His expression changes. He nods.

"He used to tell me you scared him."

What? *I* scared my *father*?

"I told him he was crazy," he says. "I said, how can a little girl scare a grown man? You know what he said?"

I shake my head.

"He said you looked like a little girl, but you were smarter than any little girl he ever knew. He said you knew things. About him."

"Mr. Dodo—"

"Edward," he says. "My name is Edward." He leans on his broom. "I remember when your daddy first came around here. He was barely walking straight. I was about to chase him away. But he had Mr. Newsome's card. He said Mr. Newsome told him to come by, he might have some work for him. I thought he was kidding—but Mr. Newsome had written the time on the back of the card—the same time your daddy showed up. So I took a chance and called in to Mr. Newsome. He hired your daddy on the spot to do what I'm doing now—keep the place clean. Especially the bathrooms." He shakes his head. "You know what a bunch of young people do to bathrooms when they're out for a night on the town?"

I could imagine.

"Your daddy did a half-assed job, if you don't mind me saying. We had a pool on him—how long he would last before Mr. Newsome finally fired him."

I hold my breath. Was that why he did it—because Mr. Newsome fired him?

"But he never did get fired," Edward says. "Bit by bit your daddy cleaned himself up. We were all surprised. It looked like Mr. Newsome had done something good for him. He showed up for work on time. He started to think about maybe bringing you up to live with him. Then it all went to hell."

"What do you mean?"

"I mean, he fell off the wagon. Got himself all hopped up again. The next thing you know, Mrs. Newsome is dead and the police get a lead on your daddy. They find him sound asleep and a whole pile of her jewelry in his room. They find a scrap of paper with the Newsomes' security code in his pocket."

"Security code?"

"Mr. Newsome had just had a security system installed at his house. The police said whoever broke in shut off the alarm."

"How did my father get the code?"

"That's the thing," Edward says. "Your daddy couldn't read without his glasses."

Glasses? I don't remember my father wearing glasses back then—and there are times, plenty of times, when I'm sure I remember every single time I ever saw him. I know it isn't possible though. No one remembers like that.

But glasses?

I would remember glasses, wouldn't I?

If I don't remember them from back then, I would remember them from all those visits. Especially the ones when I made the trip on my own. During those visits, made in the past couple of years, my father was keenly interested in my schoolwork. He actually wanted to see what I was doing. He didn't have glasses then.

I peer at the old man. He's a lot older than my father was. He's not remembering it right, I think. He's confusing my father with someone else. Or his brain is playing tricks on him. I look at the caved-in side of his head.

"But your daddy's glasses were broken," he continues when I don't speak. "He told me that. If you ask me, the miracle is how he managed to hang on to a pair of glasses as long as he did. Anyway, he never had them when he was at work. He was always asking me to check his work orders for him. Said he was going to get himself a new pair as soon as he got paid. Said that just about every week, as I recall, but he never seemed to get around to it."

"I don't think I understand..."

"That security system Mr. Newsome had, when I say it was new, I mean it was brand-new. I remember the salesman from the company he bought it from. He was down here at the club after it was installed, explaining it to Mr. Newsome. How did your daddy get the code, that's what you asked me?"

I nodded.

"They say your daddy must have seen the manual that the salesman left for Mr. Newsome. I remember Mr. Newsome talking about it. He said he'd written the code in it—he really beat himself up for that, you know, because they always tell you not to write down codes in places like that, practically the first place a person would look. Your daddy was in and out of most places in the club—kitchen, main floor, bathrooms, offices. Mr. Newsome's office. They say he must have seen that manual and seen the code written down in it, and that's how he got into the Newsome house without Mrs. Newsome even knowing he was there. The thing is, your daddy never got around to getting those glasses he needed. So you want to tell me, if he couldn't read without his glasses, how he got that code?"

I can't take my eyes off the side of his head. His eyes meet mine for a moment, and I'm ashamed to be caught staring.

"Did you tell that to anyone?" I ask.

The old man hangs his head.

"Like I said, I had my own demons back then. I didn't know anything about anything at the time except that your daddy said he done it. It wasn't until later—a lot later—that I heard what was supposed to be the real story. I called some cop, but he just laughed at me. He said your daddy took a plea, he said he did it, so don't bother him with some story about eyeglasses. But I'm telling you, that thought stayed in my head for a long time. Yes, a long time. And I still don't see it. I don't see how a man who needed eyeglasses to read but who didn't even own a pair of eyeglasses could have seen that Mr. Newsome had a manual on his desk and then go ahead and go through it and find a security code he had written in it."

"Edward, can I ask you something?"

He nods, but there's something guarded about his expression.

"The guy who brought me back here, he said you'd been in an accident."

The old man's eyes lock on mine. I see disappointment in them.

"That's true," he says.

"What happened?"

He pulls himself up straight now and holds the broom away from him, as if to show me that he doesn't have to lean on it.

"I fell," he said. "I got drunk one night and went up on the roof, and I fell." His eyes flash. "But that doesn't mean I don't remember."

"Edward, my father didn't wear glasses. Ever."

Edward's eyes refuse to let mine go.

"That's not what he told me," he says. "But you go ahead and believe whatever you want to believe. You believe that a little girl who hardly ever saw her daddy knows better than a man who worked with him every day for six weeks."

"Six weeks?" I sigh. "That's all? You knew him for six weeks ten years ago?" Before your accident, I think but don't say. Before your head got caved in.

He stares at me for a moment before turning and making his way back down the steps to the basement.

And now here I am in bed, still thinking about what Dodo said, going over it and over it, looking for something to give me hope, even though I should know better. He barely knew my father. He doesn't remember him right. His head is caved in.

It's noon before I get out of bed and make myself some instant coffee. I walk around the small apartment, looking at the secondhand furniture, the secondhand pots and pans, dishes and cutlery, trying to decide what to do with everything—leave it where it is, or pack it up and get rid of it?

In the end, I pull on some clothes and walk to the nearest grocery store, looking for boxes. They don't have any to spare. They send me to a liquor store. Empty boxes are stacked high in there. A woman at the only cash register that's open tells me to help myself.

When I get back to the apartment with the boxes, there's a phone message for me from Detective Sanders. She's left a number where I can reach her.

"Lila," she says when I call, sounding relieved to hear from me but also a little anxious. "How are you?"

"Okay."

"I wanted to give you an update," she says. "Do you want to meet for coffee?"

I tell her no. I tell her that if she has something to tell me, she can do it over the phone.

"We've closed the case," she says.

I brace myself. I know what she's going to tell me. It's no surprise, but still, I don't want to hear it.

She spells it out for me. A homicide: my father shot and killed Tracie Newsome. And an attempted homicide: he tried to kill Mr. Newsome, who struggled to defend himself, and, in that struggle, killed my father, a clear case of self-defense. She stops and waits for me to say something.

"Thanks for calling to tell me," I say. I'm not sarcastic or bitter. She's gone out of her way to be nice to me, as if she understands that I'm a person who has lost her father and, for that reason, she feels for me.

"What are you going to do now?" she asks.

The words that come out of my mouth surprise me. "I'm going back home."

As soon as I hang up, the phone rings again. It's Finn Newsome. I tell him I'm not interested, and I hang up fast. Then I go back into the front hall to get the boxes I brought back. I take them into the kitchen and start to pack the kitchen stuff.

After that, I go into my father's room. I pack up his clothes—he doesn't have many. I'll take them to the Salvation Army along with the kitchen stuff. While I'm there, I'll see if they'll take back the furniture we bought. I don't want my money back. They can have it if they'll come and get it. I decide to call the landlord, too, and ask for a refund of the last month's rent. I know he doesn't have to give it to me, but I decide to plead helpless victim. I mean, it's not my fault my father did what he did. The phone rings again. I ignore it.

There's a box sitting on the floor. It was there when I arrived with my dad. It's taped shut. My father never opened it. I pick at a corner of the tape until I can grab hold of it and rip off the whole strip. I open the box.

There are books inside. Seven of them. Three of them are slim paperbacks. I see by the covers that they are books for people who don't read English well—people who are just learning the language. Another two are books about hockey. The other two books are textbooks. Grammar books.

Underneath the grammar books are some exercise books, the thin kind that kids use in elementary school. There are nearly a dozen of them, all of them dog-eared.

Now I know why my father never opened the box. It was left here by the last tenant, who must have been an immigrant.

The doorbell rings.

I shove the box aside. Who can it be? Not Detective Sanders. I just spoke to her. Maybe it's the landlord. Maybe he's read about my dad. Maybe he's come to throw me out. After all, my name isn't on the rental agreement.

I go to the door and peek through the window.

I freeze.

It's him. It's Finn Newsome. He sees me, and he smiles at me. What is he even doing here? How does he know where I live? I want to pretend that I haven't seen him and he hasn't seen me. But I can't, not when our eyes are locked like this.

I open the door.

His eyes pop wide, as if he's surprised to see me, which I don't understand. Who was he expecting? I'm not sure what to say. So many things occur to me: *Didn't I already tell you I'm not interested? Don't you know how to listen when someone tells you something? Do you have any idea who I really am?*

But what actually comes out of my mouth is, "How did you know where to find me?"

His face turns brilliant red. He stammers.

"I—my friend John…he looked it up. Look, I'm sorry, but I just…"

He stops. He's literally tongue-tied. He's taller than me and, I hate to admit it, kind of cute. Okay, really cute. He's got black hair like his father, except that his is an unruly mass of curls. I'm guessing he got that from his mother. He has those blue eyes I noticed at the cemetery—blue like a lake in summer. And he's in good shape. But when he runs out of words and ducks his head and somehow manages to look up at me, he looks like a little kid who knows that he's done something wrong and is hoping, probably against hope, that he won't be punished for it.

But that's only part of the reason I relent. The other part is, he's here. The eyewitness to my father's shooting is right here on my doorstep.

"You want to come in?" I ask.

His head bobs up.

"Really? You mean it?"

He sounds so surprised—again—that I can't help smiling.

"Really," I say. I step aside to let him in.

Seventeen
FINN

Lila does not look happy when she opens the door. In fact, she looks as if she'd like to punch me one in the jaw. She's so small—her head just reaches my shoulder—and she's thin. But the fierce expression on her face tells me that she doesn't scare easily and that, if she felt she had to, she would attack.

"How did you know where to find me?" she demands, and right away I realize that John's idea was a lousy one. You don't just appear on the doorstep of a girl who hasn't given you her address and, more to the point, has told you that she isn't interested in speaking to you. If you ignore common sense and *do* show up, be prepared to come across like some kind of stalker.

I try to explain, but I realize that, when you get right down to it, there is no sensible explanation. She stares at me.

I feel myself turn red. I feel the heat in my cheeks. And then something happens—I have no idea what— and she invites me in.

My first thought: the place is a dive. I stare at carpets that are threadbare and stained; walls that could use a coat, preferably two, of paint; furniture that looks like it came from the Salvation Army. Then I see a couple of boxes on the kitchen table, and the kitchen cupboards, their doors open, their shelves empty. I glance at Lila.

"I'm packing," she says, and I swear she knows exactly what I'm thinking. She looks pointedly at my Frye boots that I bet cost more than a month's rent on this dump.

"You're moving?"

"I'm going back to live with my aunt in Boston."

"Oh," I say, and I realize that I'm disappointed. I don't know anything about this girl except her name and the fact that her father just died, but I'm disappointed that she's moving so far away.

"You want some tea or something?" she asks.

I glance at the boxes.

"The mugs are near the top," she says, doing it again, making me think she's reading my mind.

"Okay, sure."

She goes into the kitchen and takes a cheap kettle out of one of the boxes, fills it from the sink and sets it onto a gas burner. She pulls two mugs from the other box. They're right at the top, just like she said. There are only two of them. In fact, it looks to me that there are only two of everything.

"So it was just you and your dad here?" I say without thinking.

Now *she* stares at *me*, as if stunned by my mind-reading abilities. She nods and moves around the cramped kitchen, fishing out sugar—a handful of packets that look like they were swiped from a restaurant or coffee shop—some milk—a small container, which she sniffs—and a couple of tea bags.

The kettle boils, and she pours water over the tea bags in each mug. She sets them on the table next to the sugar packets and the milk and digs out a spoon. We fix our tea. She picks up her mug and says, "So, what is it that you want?"

I decide on the honest approach. I figure she'll see right through me if I try anything else.

"I don't know, exactly," I say. "I just...I just thought about you, about seeing you at the police station and then at the funeral, and I wanted to talk to you again."

She thinks this over and doesn't throw me out.

"You want to sit down?"

I reach for one of the kitchen chairs—metal, with a vinyl-covered padded seat—but she shakes her head.

"In there." She nods to the living room, and I follow her in. She sits on one end of a dingy brown sofa. I sit on an olive-colored armchair so I can see her.

"So, how are you doing?" she asks.

"How am *I* doing?" Her father has just died, and she's asking me how *I* am?

"You know, since your stepmother's funeral."

I'm about to say I never liked Tracie much anyway when it occurs to me that this will make me look like, well, like an asshole. I try to think of something else to say. She beats me to it.

"It must have been awful, seeing it happen."

"It was," I admit. "It was like watching a movie, only I knew it was real. And when I heard the second shots and saw the guy and my dad both go down…"

I'm not sure how it happens. One minute I'm telling her what happened. Then I flash back to the night my mom died, and I feel something burning me. Lila jumps up. That's when it registers that I must have zoned out, because I've spilled my tea. It's slopped all over my thighs and the ugly olive chair. She's out of the room and back again in a flash with a towel, which she thrusts at me, and grabs the nearly empty mug from my hand.

"Are you okay?" she asks.

I'm on my feet, doing my best to sop up the tea and ignore the burning sensation on my thighs. I press the towel down onto the chair too.

"Never mind that," she says. "It's going back to the Salvation Army."

Back to the Salvation Army?

"You went white there for a minute. Did you get burned?"

Yeah, I got burned. "I'm okay," I say. I'm also embarrassed. "Sorry about that."

"I'm the one who should be sorry. If you don't want to talk about it, it's okay. I should mind my own business."

"What? No. No, it's not your fault." That's the last thing I want her to think. I glance around for somewhere else to sit.

"You want some more tea?" she asks.

"No, really," I say quickly. I don't want to chance another accident.

She laughs at how fast I answer. Then I laugh. It feels good. And I'm struck by how different she looks when she seems happy, how much prettier, and she's already a knockout.

She gestures to the couch. I sit on one end. She sits on the other. We're both turned inward to face each other. She brings her legs up under her, and before I know it, I'm telling her about that night, about the man who came to the door earlier, about him going away again, everything my dad said about the man phoning him. I tell her about hearing my dad's voice and then Tracie's. I try not to paint Tracie as the annoying, money-obsessed ex-cocktail waitress she was. But she picks up on it anyway.

"Sounds like you didn't like her," she says.

"I didn't say that."

"But you didn't, did you?" she says.

I want to tell her she's wrong, but I can see in her eyes that she already knows the truth.

"No," I admit finally. "For a while there, I thought she and my dad were going to split up. They argued a lot. Then it blew over. But the ironic thing is, if they had split up, Tracie wouldn't have been at the house that night. She'd still be alive."

She's quiet for a long time before she finally says, "What about your mother?"

"What about her?"

"It must have been hard, losing her."

"Yeah." And then I'm talking again, saying things I've never said to anyone else. I tell her how much my dad loved my mom and how hard it was for him after she died. I tell her he loved her more than anything else in the world, and so did I. I tell her that I wasn't home that night, that I was at the club with my dad. I also tell her that I was the one who found her. And then I say something that I have never, ever in the whole ten years since my mother's death said out loud, not even to the shrink my dad sent me to.

I say, "If I'd stayed home that night, it never would have happened."

She frowned. "How do you figure that?"

"I would have heard the guy break in."

"You said it happened really late. You were seven years old. You would have been asleep. And, anyway, you said it wasn't that kind of break-in. Nobody kicked in a door or smashed a window. You said he knew the security code. There wasn't anything to hear."

"I would have heard my mom scream."

She peers at me with smoky-gray eyes. "How do you know she screamed? She was in her room, right? You said she was wearing a nightgown. She was probably asleep when the guy let himself into the house."

"She would have screamed when she saw the gun," I say. I know it. I've had ten long years to think about it. I never stopped thinking about it, and since Tracie died, it's been on my mind practically night and day.

"And then what?" she says. "You would have run into her room to see what was the matter? And if you'd seen the guy—" A funny look comes into her eyes—maybe pain, like she really cares about what she's saying. "He shot your mom. Do you think he would have let you live if you'd been able to identify him? He would have shot you too, Finn. How would that have helped?"

I stare at her. I want to tell her she's wrong. I would have heard my mother scream. I would have run to help her. I would have attacked the man. I would have wrestled the gun from him. I would have saved her. She'd be alive right now.

"You were a little kid," she says again. "He was a grown man."

"But I—" But I what? I would have turned into Superman? I would have tackled the guy to the ground? I've seen him close up. I saw him the other night. He wasn't just a grown man. He was a big man—taller than me and bulky. There was no way I would have been able to bring him down. I'd have a hard enough time now. But when I was seven? I can't shake the memory of my mother, and of all that blood. I also think about all the years since then—the emptiness, the grief, the missing, the longing. "Then I would have been shot," I say finally. "But I would have done *something*. I would have at least tried. She deserved to have somebody there. She deserved to have someone try, after everything she'd been through."

"What do you mean?" she asks.

I've thought about my mother a million times over the years, but none of it has been as vivid as it is now that I'm talking about her, now that I'm trying to explain her and her death and my feelings—everything—to someone, to a stranger, out loud. It's as if I've thrown open a window and I have no control over what I see out there right in front of my eyes. And for some reason that I can't explain, I want to tell her. I want to tell Lila.

"She wasn't happy," I say. "She was tired a lot."

"Was she sick?"

"I don't think so." I realize that I don't actually know. "She told my dad she needed some time alone."

"You mean, like a trial separation or something?"

"*What?*" Where did she get that idea? "No! No, she was just tired, that's all."

Lila stares at me. She's thinking something, but I can tell she's not going to come out and say it.

"She loved my dad," I tell her, just to make it perfectly clear. "She married him even though her mother was against it. She was a snob. My grandmother, I mean. She thought my dad wasn't good enough for her daughter. But my mother didn't listen. She married him. She helped him with his club. It was his big dream, and she backed him every step of the way."

"Okay," she says. But her eyes say something different. She's agreeing with me so that I'll stay calm. She doesn't want an angry stranger in her crappy little house.

"Damn straight, okay!" I say. "You don't know anything about my parents. She loved my dad. Why would she want a separation?" Except that now that Lila said it, I hear voices, hushed but angry. I see my mother glance through a doorway and see me and then reach out and close the door before continuing to talk to my father, still in a hushed voice. I hear them at night, long after I've gone to bed, probably when my father gets in from the club. "She loved him."

"Okay," she says again in that same tone of voice. She's not agreeing with me. She's placating me, using the word to try to calm me down. *Okay, sure, anything you say.*

I'm on my feet, and, boy, am I angry.

"You don't know what you're talking about," I shout at her.

Her feet slide out from under her. She leans forward a little and looks up at me.

"I didn't mean anything by it," she says. "I was just trying—"

"I don't care what you were trying to do." Why did I even come here? What was I thinking? I don't know this girl. I don't know anything about her. For all I know, she's some kind of ghoul who gets off on funerals and the grief of others. "I have to go."

I'm out of the living room and then out the front door before she can get off the couch to stop me—assuming she even wanted to stop me. Maybe she's glad that I'm leaving. After all, she never wanted to see me in the first place.

Eighteen
LILA

I never wanted him there, but he tracked me down anyway. At first I was scared. At first I thought he knew who I was. But he doesn't. He doesn't ask me for my full name. He doesn't ask for my father's name. Or maybe he thinks he knows. He said his friend looked up our phone number; that's how he found the address. But the phone isn't in my name or my dad's name. It's in the name of the last person who lived here and who forgot to tell the phone company he was moving. My father had it on his to-do list: inform the phone company. But he never got around to it. In fact, he'd been thinking it over. Why not just pay the bill when it came and keep the phone. That way, we'd avoid any special connection fee, which, my father said, usually involved a credit check, which he probably wouldn't pass.

Finn doesn't know who I am, but I know who he is. That means I have a chance to find out what happened.

Except I don't keep my mouth shut, which would have been the smart thing. Instead, I decide to ask questions and give unasked-for opinions. In other words, I blow it. He freaks out when I ask if his mother wanted to separate from his father. Well, that's what it sounded like to me. What else does a woman mean when she tells her husband she needs time alone? But then, who asked me? I shouldn't have said anything.

I sip my tea. I'm angry at myself for having the chance to learn something and finding out exactly nothing— well, except that maybe the first Mrs. Newsome was giving some thought to the future of her marriage, no matter what Finn thinks. He was seven years old at the time. What seven-year-old wants to think his parents are going to break up?

What else do I know now that I didn't know before? Nothing useful. His grandmother was against the marriage. I wonder what she had against Finn's father. I want to know because I want to have something against him too. He killed my father. I want to hate him for that instead of hating my father for going over there with a gun and trying to kill him...assuming that was his intention. I keep thinking about Detective Sanders's question: *Did he say anything to you about money, Lila?* According to Finn, he said something to Mr. Newsome about it. It's why he went there in the first place.

I set my mug down on the floor and push myself up off the couch. I go into the dingy little room that I've been trying to think of as my bedroom, even though it isn't as nice as my room at Aunt Jenny's and contains hardly any of my stuff. Most of that is still back home.

Back home. Where I mostly grew up. Where I belong now.

I look around the room. I should just finish packing and get out of here. I have enough money for a bus ticket. I don't need to stay here any longer.

I open the top drawer of a cheap chest of drawers. I feel under my socks and underwear and pull out a file folder. I take it back into the living room with me, sit down and open it. The folder contains everything I know about my father's case, which isn't much. As soon as he was arrested, I was taken by child welfare. They contacted my aunt, and the next thing I knew, I was far away. Aunt Jenny tried to shield me from what was happening, which turned out to be easy. People in Boston weren't interested in something that had happened far away to someone who wasn't a native Bostonian and who hadn't lived in Boston for more than a few months. So the folder was pretty thin—a few clippings and a few things I found on the Internet a little later.

It consisted of the following:

An obituary for the first Mrs. Newsome—Angela Fairlane Newsome. There was a picture. I hadn't looked at it in years, but when I pull out the clipping with the little black-and-white photo, I am stunned to see how much Finn resembles his mother. According to the article, Angela Fairlane was daughter to Albert Finn Fairlane, an eccentric Ivy Leaguer who quit a lucrative law practice to turn inventor and who made a fortune when he patented some gizmos that most people have never heard of but that are used in manufacturing processes all over the world. Angela came from money. She was also an Ivy Leaguer. But, the obituary said, she became a devoted mother to her only son Finn. In other words, she didn't put that Ivy League education to work. At least, not on a job or career of her own. The obituary also noted that she was both a helpmate and business partner to her "beloved husband Robert."

I see a couple of articles about the burglary and shooting, short items that I had found in Aunt Jenny's house one day after school. They didn't say much, only that Angela Newsome, a thirty-year-old homemaker, was dead after being shot during a break-and-enter at her home on a quiet tree-lined street in an affluent neighborhood. The police suspected that she had surprised a burglar. A follow-up article noted that an arrest had been made and mentioned that Mrs. Newsome's body had been discovered by her seven-year-old son. A final article quoted Mr. Newsome as saying that he was "devastated" by his wife's murder and that he wished that he and his son had stayed home that night instead of going to his place of business, a popular dance club. If they had been home, he said, the burglary and murder never would have happened. He also noted the bitter irony that he had just installed a security system that, somehow, the killer had managed to disable.

Finally, a three-inch-long article about my father's court date, plea and conviction that noted Mr. Newsome's outrage that he had been offered ten to life instead of straight life and his fervent hope that no parole board in the country would ever consider my father for release.

I read each article over twice, and for the first time I consider, really consider, what it must have been like for a seven-year-old boy to find his mother dead in her own bedroom. I consider also what memories must have been prompted by seeing a second murder—the murder of his stepmother—at the hands of the same person who murdered his mother.

I feel sorry for Finn. I really do.

But instead of packing up the rest of my things, instead of calling the landlord and arranging to see him so that I can plead for the refund of the last month's rent, instead of calling the Salvation Army to see if they will pick up the things I have for them or at least help me get them to their store, instead of any of that, I grab my bag and head out the door.

I have to ask five different people before I find someone who can direct me to the nearest library. When I get there, I find I need a library card if I want to sign up to use a computer. I have a local address, so I go ahead and pay a dollar and get a card. I sign up and am told that I will have to wait an hour before a computer is free. No problem. I wait. When my name is finally called, I log on to the Internet and type in my father's name. I find several longer articles about him from the newspaper. I print them out. Then I type in Robert Newsome's name. A lot more information pops up. I scan it and print out the articles that seem the most interesting. Angela Fairlane's name brings up a couple more articles. Her father's name gets me dozens of pages. I scan again and print out the three that have the most information. The only thing that Tracie Newsome's name hits is an engagement notice.

I go to the library desk to retrieve my printing, at ten cents a page. Then I sit down and start to read. I read everything twice. But it doesn't help. Nothing helps. No matter how hard I try, I can't change the facts. I can't make my father anything but a murderer, no matter what he told me and no matter what Dodo remembers or thinks he does.

Nineteen
FINN

I'm almost home by the time I calm down, and then I feel like a fool. A complete idiot. I went over there to see her and talk to her. I told myself that it was the right thing to do; after all, she lost her father. But did I ask her about that? Did I ask her about what happened? Did I say or do anything to make her feel better?

No.

Instead, I talked about myself one hundred percent of the time. And then I yelled at her. Nice going. Go to someone else's place, accept her hospitality, spill tea all over her furniture, and then ream her out for something that has nothing to do with her.

I don't just feel like an idiot. I *am* an idiot.

I let myself into the house. It's quiet, but I know my

dad has to be home because his car is sitting out in front of the garage.

I hear something upstairs.

I go to see what it is. The clothes bags are where I left them, but all of them have been opened and everything inside them is jumbled up and looks like it's been taken out and then stuffed back in instead of folded neatly the way I'd done.

The door to my dad's room is open too. I peek inside, but I don't see my dad.

I hear something again. Muttering. I take a step across the threshold and find my dad on his hands and knees in Tracie's walk-in closet.

"Dad?"

He straightens up so fast that he whacks his head against the underside of a shelf. He curses as he spins around.

"Finn. You gave me a scare."

He brushes off the knees of his pants. They're his good clothes, the ones he wears to business meetings and to the club. He usually changes out of them as soon as he gets home from work. He's usually pretty fastidious about keeping his clothes in good shape.

"What are you doing, Dad?"

"Just checking," he says.

"I cleaned out all of Tracie's things for you."

"So I see." His eyes are darting all over the now-empty dressing room.

"Is something wrong, Dad?"

His eyes jump back to me.

"Wrong?" he says. "What do you mean?"

"I bagged all of Tracie's things. I folded them up all neatly and everything. But it looks like someone went through them. Were you looking for something?"

"Some jewelry," he says.

"Jewelry?" Tracie had a lot of jewelry. Some of it is stuff she owned before she married my dad. It's costume jewelry. Junk. It isn't worth anything. My dad bought her some things—an engagement ring and a wedding ring, of course, and a couple of bracelets and earrings for her birthday or for anniversaries or at Christmas.

Then there's the other stuff—the stuff that made me want to strangle her every time I saw her wearing it. It's my mother's jewelry. A lot of it belonged to *her* mother or her grandmother. Beautiful rings and bracelets, necklaces and earrings, all of it worth a lot of money. That's the stuff that was stolen the night my mother died. The police recovered all of it, every single piece. They told my dad he was lucky. Ever since then, my dad has kept it in a safe hidden in his closet. Closing the barn door after the horse has left, he said when the men came to install it. But he's not taking any chances with my mother's jewelry. It's there when Tracie isn't—wasn't—wearing it. She didn't know the combination. I guess he wasn't taking any chances with her either.

"Some earrings are missing," my father says. "I thought maybe she dropped them somewhere in here.

You didn't see them when you were cleaning out her clothes, did you?"

I shake my head.

"Were they valuable?" I ask.

"They belonged to your grandmother."

And there it is—that feeling that used to roil up inside me whenever I saw Tracie wearing something that used to belong to my mother. Only now I'm looking at my dad and feeling it.

"You're kidding, right?" I say.

My dad's face fills with regret.

"They're around somewhere. She knew how valuable they were. I'm sure she was careful—"

"You just said you thought she dropped them in here. Dropping stuff isn't being careful with it, Dad." I'm yelling at him. I'm yelling at my dad, who just lost his wife.

He raises his hands. "Take it easy, son."

I want to take it easy. I know I shouldn't be yelling at him. But I can't stop.

"I can't believe you even let her have them in the first place. They were Mom's. They belonged to her. Grandma gave them to her."

"That's why I'm looking for them, Finn," my dad says calmly.

"You wouldn't have to look for them if you hadn't let her wear them," I say, furious. "Besides, they weren't yours to give. But you did anyway. You gave them to Tracie—"

I spit out her name, as if it's something poisonous in my mouth. "You gave them to Tracie, and now look what happened."

I'm breathing hard. My hands are curled at my sides. All the resentment I felt when he started seeing Tracie, all the contempt I felt for Tracie when she was alive, all the evil, bad things I thought about my dad for even being attracted to her, let alone having married her, comes spilling out. She wasn't as smart as Mom. She didn't care about other people the way Mom did. She spent too much time thinking about how she looked and what other people thought about her. She tried too hard to be sexy.

"Finn, settle down." There's an edge to my dad's voice.

"She used to walk around in her underwear, Dad, and she didn't care who saw her. She didn't care if *I* saw her. She was a tramp. I hated her."

I stop as soon as that last sentence is out of my mouth. I stare at my dad. Every muscle in my body tenses involuntarily, and I wait because I am sure my dad is going to hit me.

He steps forward.

I brace myself.

His arms come out.

I know I deserve whatever happens next.

But he doesn't hit me. Instead, he throws his arms around me and pulls me to him. He holds me tightly, and the next thing I know, I am crying.

"I'm sorry, Dad. I didn't mean that. I'm sorry..."

"It's okay, Finn," he says. His voice is soft and soothing. He doesn't let me go. "I know how you felt about her. You didn't know her like I did. It's okay. I love you, son."

When I finally pull away from him, I can see that his eyes are watery too, but I don't know if his tears are for me or for Tracie.

"We'll get through this," he says. "We've been through it before, and we can do it again. We're going to be okay. You believe me, don't you, Finn?"

I nod.

"Come on. Let's go downstairs and get some supper."

"I'm not hungry, Dad." I haven't been hungry since this whole thing started.

"Neither am I," my dad says. "But we have to eat. Come on."

He closes the closet door and throws an arm around me. We head down to the kitchen, where my dad pulls out everything he needs to make bacon and eggs—it's what he calls his specialty. While he's frying the bacon, I say, "Did you and Mom ever think about getting separated?"

My dad's back is to me as he stands at the stove, but he looks over his shoulder.

"Separated? Whatever gave you that idea?"

"I don't know." That's not true. I know exactly what— *who*—gave me that idea. "I've been thinking about Mom since Tracie died. Thinking about that night, you know?"

"I know," my dad says quietly. He turns back to the stove.

"I think I remember that you and Mom used to argue a lot."

"All married couples argue sometimes, Finn."

"I know. But it seems like you were arguing a lot before Mom…before she died. And I think I remember her saying that she needed some time alone."

My dad's back is still to me. He cracks four eggs, one by one, into a bowl, and then pours them into the frying pan with the bacon.

"That's why I took you to the club that night," he says. "Because your mother was tired and wanted some downtime." He turns again, smiling gently, as if he's afraid that what he is going to say might hurt me. And, sure enough, it does. "It wasn't time away from me that she wanted, Finn. It was time away from you. You were a real handful when you were little, and your mom was here alone with you every night while I was at the club. That's why I started to take you with me. That's why I took you with me that night, even though it was a school night. So your mom could have some downtime. So she wouldn't have to deal with you."

I stare at him. I can't think of a single thing to say to that. It doesn't even make me feel good to know for sure that Lila was wrong and I was right, because now I start remembering me at five years old and six years old and seven years old. I was always getting into something, and my mom was always telling me, "Finn, can't you sit still for five minutes?"

My dad slides two plates of bacon and eggs onto the table along with a stack of toast. He sits down opposite me.

"Eat," he says.

And I do, even though I'm not even remotely hungry. I eat because I don't want to drive my father as crazy as I apparently drove my mother. I don't say another word. Instead, I listen to my dad tell me how things are going at the club. I think I even manage to look interested in every word.

Twenty
LILA

As far as the police are concerned, it's case closed—twice. I want them to be wrong, but I know they're not. I think about my father. I think about what he did and what he told the police he did ten years ago (a theft and a killing he said he didn't even remember, when he finally confessed to it) and what he told me he did. ("Nothing, I swear it. I'm going to make it up to you, Lila. We're going to be a family again—I swear it.") I think about the other wives and children, the mothers and sisters and girlfriends who sat on the bus with me on my way to visit my father, who checked into the motels around the prison, who lined up and went through searches and filled out forms so that they could go and sit in the same room I sat in and listen to their husbands and fathers, their sons and brothers and boyfriends tell them the same thing my father told me:

"It's all a mistake, I swear it. Everything is going to be different once I get out of here, I swear it. I'm going to make it up to you. I swear it."

I think about the statistics. The numbers. I know them because my Aunt Jenny studied up on them and passed them along to me. "I'm not trying to hurt you, Lila," she'd say. "But I think you should be realistic. I think everyone should be realistic. And the fact is…"

The fact is that people like my father, people who start along the wrong path early in life, usually find their way back to that same wrong path, no matter how good their intentions might be, every once in a while.

"For people like your father," Aunt Jenny would say, "the easy way is the way they always drift toward. They can't help it. It's all they know."

The easy way.

Detective Sanders: "Did he say anything to you about needing money, Lila?"

And there it is.

My fault.

Because even though he didn't say it, the fact is, he needed money.

"You're going to go back to school, Lila," he said to me. He said it over and over, when he was still locked up. "You're going to be the first one in my family to graduate high school. You're going to be the first one to go to university. You're going to be the first one to make something of herself."

"Yes, Dad."

I studied. I did. But I also held down a job because... because I felt bad about being a burden on Aunt Jenny, even though she never complained about it. I felt bad about having to rely on her. I felt bad that she did what she did for me out of a sense of duty to my mother, her baby sister, and not because it was a choice she would have made otherwise. I felt bad that my father was such a screwup. I felt bad that he was in prison and everyone knew it. I felt bad asking Aunt Jenny to take me to see him; it cost money for the bus, money for the motel, money to take him things to make him happy. I felt bad all the time, and the only way to feel better was to make my own way.

So I did.

I'm making my own way now.

But working at one thing—a job—means less time to work at other things, like school.

And less time to work at school means lower grades.

It's like that story about the battle being lost because one single horse lost a shoe. You know: For want of a nail, the shoe was lost. For want of a shoe, the horse was lost. For want of a horse, the rider was lost. For want of a rider, the battle was lost. For want of a battle, the kingdom was lost. And all for the want of a horseshoe nail.

I didn't do well enough to get a scholarship.

And because I felt bad about that—because I spent my whole life feeling bad—I told my father. I *confessed.*

You see, I'm no better than you, Dad. That's what I was thinking, even if I didn't come right out and say the words. I'm no better than you. I made a promise, but I didn't keep it. I chose to do something else instead. And I knew, every day while I was doing that something else, where it was going to lead. Just like you, Dad, when you made the wrong choice every day. I knew what I was doing. I knew where it would lead. I knew it would mean that I couldn't keep my promise. But I did it anyway.

I'm just like you.

I am my father's daughter.

And because I didn't keep my promise, and because I didn't keep my mouth shut but felt I had to confess, I pushed you too. No scholarship means no money to make your dream come true. *Your* dream, Dad, not mine—that's what I want to say. But saying that is just a way of shifting the blame off me and onto you. I don't want to do that.

So, because I didn't keep my promise, because I disappointed you, you slipped too. You fell off the path of good intentions and onto the path called the Easy Way. You wanted money, for me. I know it was for me. You wanted the money to make your dream come true—to make me be the one, the very first one in your family, to amount to something. It doesn't matter how you get what you want, right, Dad? You need something you don't have, you know someone else who has it, so you take it.

Or try to.

But when Mr. Newsome refused to hand it over, then what?

Detective Sanders: *"Did he say anything to you about needing money, Lila?"*

Me: *"No."*

A lie.

I'm just like you. I break promises. I tell lies. I take the easy way. I tell myself I lied to Detective Sanders to protect you, but that's not true. I lied because I'm tired of being the daughter of a killer.

And now, like you, I surrender. There's nothing more I can do except go back home to Aunt Jenny and admit to her that she was right and I was wrong and maybe—*maybe*—find the strength to try again to do the right thing. Go back to school. Try to ignore what people will think, now that my father is a two-time killer. Focus myself. Study. Make something of my life. Aunt Jenny will tell me that it's time I finally did something for myself. But is that what I'm doing?

Is it?

I drop by the Salvation Army on my way home and tell them that I have a bunch of stuff that I want to donate to them but that some of it is furniture and I don't have any way to get it to them. The lady there is nice. She tells me they can send a truck to pick the stuff up. She asks for my address and tells me someone will be by the next day.

I go back to the flat and finish packing the kitchen stuff. I dust and clean off the battered old furniture as best I can.

I call the landlord and leave a message for him to call me. I get the box of my father's things from "his" room, the one he slept in exactly twice, and add it to the boxes from the kitchen. I pick up the second box from my father's room, the box of books left behind by a previous tenant. I take it out back to the alley behind the row of rental houses, each with several apartments in it. There are mini-Dumpsters back there for garbage, and big plastic containers for recycling. I flip open the top of the big recycling container for paper and cardboard. It's empty, but not for long. I tip the box from my father's room into it. he books fall first. Then the notebooks. Then...

I stare down into the recycling container.

I drop the empty box and lean down, reaching inside.

I pull out the last thing that fell into the container—a photograph. It's an eight-by-ten full-color picture. Of me, age nine. Taken at school. What's my photo doing in a box that belongs to a complete stranger?

I reach into the recycling container again. There are more photographs, all of me, all at different ages. Every year a photographer would come to my school and take individual pictures of every kid. Every year we would take order sheets home. You could buy packages— so many little pictures, so many slightly larger pictures, so many big ones. Every year Aunt Jenny bought a package. And every year when Aunt Jenny would take me (against her better judgment, she always said) to see my father, I would take one of the big pictures for him.

There I am at age nine, and again at age ten. Then eleven and twelve…Inside the bin is every picture of me that I ever gave my father. I can see from the back of each one that they were fastened to the wall with tape. I start to cry.

It takes me awhile to settle down again and to think. What are my pictures doing in this box?

There is only one explanation.

The box belongs to my father.

I dig deep into the recycling container and pull everything out—the slim paperbacks and the books about hockey. My father was a hockey nut. He followed the Montreal Canadiens his whole life, even when he was inside. He knew all the players and all their strengths and weaknesses. He idolized the ones who were French-Canadian. My father was born in Quebec.

The grammar books.

And the exercise books.

I flip one open and stare at what I see inside. I page through the whole book. Then the next one and the next one. I feel a chill run through me as I stand in the alley alone, flipping from page to page, staring, reading my father's stories about his days in prison, his struggle with drugs, his remembrances of his daughter—me—when I was a little girl.

I realize how little I knew about my father and how many secrets he took with him when he died. I wonder if he would have shared them with me if things had been different.

I put my hand in my pocket. The neatly folded piece of paper is still there. I pull it out and unfold it.

Twenty-One

FINN

My father goes back to the club after supper. I slouch in front of the TV and don't answer my phone when it rings, even though it's John calling. I know what he wants. He wants to ask why I haven't been to school and how I made out with the girl—neither of which I want to talk about. Sooner or later the school will call my dad and ask when I'm coming back. My dad will find out I've been skipping. But I know how to play that one—with trauma and maybe a little grief. The first part at least will be true. But it isn't the trauma of seeing Tracie and that man shot dead in my driveway. It's older than that—and newer. It's the trauma of seeing my mother lying in all that blood in her bedroom, half forgotten (but never completely forgotten) and dredged up again by the latest shooting. And it's the trauma of what my dad has just told me—

it wasn't him she wanted a break from, it was me. All this time I've been thinking, if only I'd been home that night. Now I find out why I wasn't. She didn't want me there. The whole thing really is my fault. If I'd been a better kid...If I'd listened...If I'd paid attention when she told me to...

I stare right through the TV screen. I don't have a clue what's on. I don't care.

Instead, I see my mother, like a ghost. She's right there in front of me, wearing one of the little black dresses she liked when she went out for the evening with my dad. She has her hair swept up, and she's wearing gold around her neck and on her fingers and around her wrists and in her ears. I see her as if she's really there, but she isn't. If I were to stretch out my hand to touch her, my hand would go right through her, and then she'd vanish like a wisp of smoke, never there in the first place, leaving behind only those gold earrings floating in the air to remind me how angry I am that they're gone.

It was bad enough that Tracie wore them. But to lose them?

I want to hit something. Rip something. Destroy something.

I push myself up off the couch and go up to my dad's room. Like Tracie, he has his own closet, which Tracie used to call his dressing room. It's got all his suits in there, hung up neatly. It's got his shoes on rows of low shelves. It's got shelves of sweaters and jeans, shirts and T-shirts. It's got little drawers of socks and underwear.

And, behind a mirror, it's got the safe.

I hinge the mirror back and look at the round door of the safe with its combination lock. My father thinks I don't know the combination, but I do. I found out by accident one day after my mother died, when I was snooping around. The men had come to install the safe, and I heard my dad joking with one of them that he had a combination that would not only keep the jewelry safe from robbers but also from "my second wife." He'd laughed, and the workmen had laughed with him. I figured out the combination pretty fast. I started with my birthday. Then I tried my mom's. The safe popped open. But I never told him.

I reach out for the cold steel of the combination dial now. I twist it around one way, then back the other, then around again. It opens. I turn on the light over the safe and reach inside for the boxes of velvet-lined jewelry. I pull them out and open them, ready to inventory what's there, ready to make sure Tracie didn't lose anything else that she had no right wearing in the first place. I know every piece by heart. When I was little and my mother was getting ready to go out, I used to watch her try things on and choose what went best with whatever she was planning to wear or wherever she was planning to go.

I open the first box and lift out the pieces one by one—the gold, the silver, the diamonds, the rubies, the emeralds and, my favorite, the sapphires that sparkled like my mom's eyes. Everything is there.

Everything is in the next box too. And the next.

And—I don't understand it—in the last box.

Everything.

Including the earrings that my father was looking for in Tracie's closet. They're right there in their little velvet compartment, where they lived when they weren't on Tracie's ears.

I start to reach into my pocket for my cell phone to tell my dad the good news.

Then I see that there is something else in the safe—something that wasn't there the last time I looked. An envelope. I reach in and pull it out. That's when I find out it's actually two envelopes, both addressed from my dad, both from the same place. I open the first one and read it. I put it back and open the second one. I read that too.

Then I put everything back exactly where I found it, and I close the safe.

I stand there for a long time before I swing the mirror back into place, hiding the safe again. I look at my reflection, at the shell-shocked expression on my face. I don't know how long it is before I leave my father's room and go back downstairs. I do know that it's a long time before I take out my phone and dial my dad's number at the club.

"Hello?" His voice is impatient. I hear music pulsing in the background.

"Dad, it's me—"

"What?" He sounds surprised. "Finn? Hang on a sec." What I hear next is muffled, which is how I know that there is someone else in his office with him.

"...dark hair," the other voice is saying. I'm pretty sure it's one of the bouncers. "Cute. She was at the funeral. Maybe you saw her." I miss the next bit. "...to Dodo. Said she was asking about Mrs. Newsome. I thought you'd want to know..."

My dad's voice cuts in, crisp and clear.

"Finn, I'll call you back, okay?"

Before I can say anything, all I hear is dead air.

Minutes tick by, and I think he's forgotten me. He gets preoccupied by work. My mother used to complain about it. Then my phone rings.

"What's up, son?"

"It's nothing," I say. But that's not true. "They should have told you, Dad."

"Who? What's going on?" There it is, that hint of impatience, although I know he's trying for my sake to keep it under control.

"The parole board. If they'd let you know—"

I hear something else. A noise. But I can't identify it.

"Finn, I know you're having a hard time with all this. But do you think it can keep until I get home? I'll try to get away early. We'll have breakfast together. What do you say?"

"Dad, I just—"

"I gotta go, son. I'll see you when I get home. I promise."

I hear dead air.

Twenty-Two
LILA

I fly from the house as soon as I hang up the phone. I tell myself, if I don't hurry, I'll be late. First I am walking fast. Then I am jogging. Then I break into a run. People turn to look at me as I speed past them. A hundred questions and regrets are spinning around in my head. Maybe if I run fast enough, I will leave them behind.

But, of course, I don't.

The whole time I'm running, I think about Finn Newsome. It was a mistake to give him my phone number, just like it was a mistake to make this latest call.

Or was it?

I knew what I was doing when I recited my phone number, just like I knew what I was doing when I went to that funeral. I wanted to talk to him. I wanted him to tell me exactly what he saw. But then what happened?

I made a mess of it when he turned up at my door. All I succeeded in doing was upsetting him. I didn't get a chance to ask him what I'd wanted to.

Okay, that's not the truth—not the whole of it anyway.

The truth is that I chickened out. I was afraid what he would think if I started asking about that night and about what had happened to his mother all those years ago.

The truth is that I was afraid how he would react when he found out who *I* am, that I'm the daughter of the man who killed both his mother and his stepmother. I was afraid this complete stranger would hate me.

I arrive at the coffee shop out of breath and fifteen minutes early and sit down. As my breath returns to normal, I tell myself I should just stop and go home. But I don't. I'm getting good at telling myself to do one thing and then ignoring myself and doing the opposite. More truth: I spent most of my childhood with kids and grown-ups whispering behind my back: *Poor Lila, her dad is in prison. He killed a woman.* What will they say now? I don't want to know.

I take a seat at a small table near the front of the restaurant where there's no chance that he will miss me, although, really, why would he? He agreed to meet me. He seemed glad that I called. He was the one who suggested the place. He also told me not to worry, he remembers what I look like.

I'm telling myself to take long slow breaths that will trick my body into thinking everything is okay, but even so,

I'm practically jumping out of my skin from nervousness. I'm meeting an honest-to-god ex-con. I realize I don't even know what he was charged with or how long he was in there. He could be an ax murderer. Or some kind of psycho pervert. Or—another possibility—maybe he's lying about knowing my father. The possibilities rattle around in my head, and I tell myself that if I was smart, I'd get out of there. Right now. Instead, when the waitress comes around, I order a coffee, which is pretty much the last thing I need. I'm stirring it around and around when he comes through the door. Peter Struthers.

He spots me right away, smiles and comes over to my table. He sits. The waitress comes back again, and he orders a coffee.

"How are you doing, Lila?" he says. His smile looks genuine and warm. But so what? I watch TV just like anyone else. I know that psychos can come across as normal. Even better than normal—they can come across as sincere.

"I'm okay," I say. I take a sip of coffee to cover my nervousness, but it doesn't work. My hand shakes, and coffee slops onto the table.

Peter Struthers mops it up with a paper napkin.

"You want something to eat?" he asks.

I shake my head.

He studies me.

"Have you eaten anything today? Because I know how hard it can be after losing a loved one..."

I haven't eaten. I've barely slept. I guess that's why I snap. That, and the fact that I hate it when people tell me they know how I feel when *I* know for a fact that they don't.

"How exactly do you know my dad?" I say. I sound like a real bitch, but at that moment I don't care.

His eyes jump wide for a moment. He's taken aback. But all he says is, "I was a volunteer in a prison program."

I have to hand it to him; he's said the last thing I expected to hear.

"Volunteer?" For god's sake, I tell myself. Just spit it out, the question you've been dying to ask: what were you in for?

"My regular job is teaching—adult education," he says. "At the time I met your dad, I was dating a social worker." There's that gentle smile again. "She's my wife now. She was the one who got me into the volunteer program."

I'm staring at him like he's just climbed out of a spaceship and is waggling his little green antennae at me.

"You're a *teacher*?" I say.

"Yes." He's puzzled by my puzzlement. Then he smiles. "Oh," he says. "You thought I was—"

"I'm sorry." I cut him off. I don't want to hear him say what I was thinking. I don't think I could stand to sound so stupid.

"It's okay. I should have done a better introduction. But it wasn't exactly the best time, you know?"

I sure do.

"Anyway, it was through volunteering that I met your dad. By the time he finally decided to join my group, he was pretty determined to make a big change in his life."

"What kind of change?" I ask.

He frowns and leans back in his chair. The way he's looking at me makes me feel like the dumbest person on the planet.

"He decided he wanted to learn to read and write."

I stare in astonishment at Peter Struthers. I shake my head. We can't be talking about the same person.

"My father was Louis Ouimette," I say.

He nods. His eyes lock onto mine, and I see that they're the same gray as a stormy sky.

"He had you fooled, huh?" he says.

"Fooled? I don't understand. My father was French-Canadian. He—"

"He used that as his cover. Or he'd say he'd broken his glasses and hadn't gotten around to getting them replaced."

Again with the glasses! He reminds me of Dodo—and neither of them knows what they're talking about.

"My father was born in Quebec," I say angrily. "In the north. He lived there until—"

He raises a hand in surrender.

"I'm doing a lousy job at communicating," he says. "I don't mean that I didn't think your father was really French-Canadian. I just meant that he used that to cover the fact that he was functionally illiterate—in any language."

Illiterate?

"Not *my* father," I say. "My father put a high value on education. He was always telling me it was the most important thing." But I'm thinking about the box I found, which is the reason I called Peter Struthers in the first place. And even as I'm practically yelling the words at him, I realize that he isn't the person I'm angry with. He just happens to be the only person around I can yell at.

He stays perfectly calm.

"Your dad put a high value on education because his own lack of it had a big impact on his life, Lila. It took him a long time to realize it, but he did. I taught your father for the past few years. When he was first recommended for the class, he refused. He wouldn't even admit that he needed to learn. Then something changed. He told me it was you. He said he realized that he was going to get out one day and he wanted to make a life with you. I think that's what made him change his mind. He didn't want you to think he was stupid."

"Why would I think that? My father wasn't stupid. He had problems. But he knew a lot of stuff. He could fix anything. And he could make things. Anything."

Peter Struthers nods. "It's been my experience that people who are functionally illiterate are very clever about hiding it. And they compensate by developing other skills. People like your dad, who function pretty well without being able to read and write, can develop good memories. And, in your dad's case, he had good spatial abilities. Once he made up his mind and got over the impatience that adults often experience when learning what they think of as kid stuff, he did really well. Grammar drove him crazy, but he applied himself. He did it for you, Lila."

My mind is racing. I want to tell him he's wrong about my father.

"You're saying my father really was illiterate?"

"Functionally illiterate. And the key word is *was*. To all intents and purposes, he couldn't read and write when he went into prison. But he could when he got out. That's what I wanted to tell you. He used to write to me from time to time. I know he never told you. He was too ashamed. But I think it was a great thing that he did. And he did it for you more than for himself. I know he's had a rough life. I also know that you loved him. I thought you would be happy to know what he did for you. Happy and proud."

Tears dribble down my cheeks as I think about what he's just told me. I remember my mother reading to me when I was small, before she died. But never my father. He used to watch TV with me. And sports. And sometimes movies. But he never read to me. And now that I think about it, I can't remember ever seeing him with a book. Or a newspaper. And he was always too busy—so he said—to go to my school to meet my teachers.

And then he was in prison.

"But I used to write to him."

"He got the prison chaplain to read your letters to him. It was the chaplain who asked me to talk to him about enrolling in my class. He turned me down at first."

"He never wrote to me."

"He couldn't bring himself to tell someone else to write what was in his heart, not even the chaplain. And, anyway, he knew you would never stop writing— or visiting."

"I never did."

"I know."

"But he learned," I say.

"He struggled, and he learned. And then he started to read. He enjoyed it."

"I found some books about hockey."

Peter Struthers smiled. "I used to tease him. I used to tell him he already knew everything there was to know about hockey and that he should find a new subject to become an expert on. I liked your dad, Lila. I wanted to tell you that. He was smart and funny, and he was doing really well. Once he got settled, we were going to talk about getting him into some training, you know, so he could get a better job. But—" His voice trails off, and he doesn't have to explain why. He never had the chance to get together with my father. And now he never would.

We talk for a while longer. When we finally leave the café, Peter Struthers says, "If there's anything I can do, Lila, if you need anything, Janet and I would be happy to see what we can do."

I thank him. Then I tell him that I will be going home soon to my Aunt Jenny. He nods and tells me he's heard she's a good person. My dad must have told him that.

* * *

My hands are shaking as I pick up the first of what I now know are my father's notebooks. I'm sitting at the kitchen table, a mug of tea at my elbow. It takes a few moments before I can make myself focus on the cramped, almost reluctant, handwriting on the first page. And then I start to read.

My father has written down what he remembers of his father, who I never met. I always thought he was dead. But he isn't. Or, at least, he wasn't when my father wrote about him. He was living in a cabin somewhere in the bush in northern Quebec, where he's apparently been ever since his wife, my grandmother, died before I was even born. As I read, I try to picture my father as a child, living with his man who was his father, this man who, according to my father, never amounted to much and resented the world for it. *I do not know what my père wanted to be when he was a boy*, my father wrote. *Did he want to be rich? Did he want to be successful? Or did he want to be the mean bastard that he really was?*

I stare at that line and understand why my father never spoke about his father. I understand, too, why my father couldn't read and write.

Trapping, fishing and hunting was his life, my father wrote. *He made it my life too, even though I hated it. I hated to see the foxes and rabbits dead or dying in leg-hold traps. I hated killing them if they weren't dead already and skinning them. I hated all the blood. My père called me a sissy. I hated pulling the fish out of the water and bashing their brains in. I hated pointing a rifle at a deer and pulling the trigger. I hated that that was the way he lived and ate. Most of all, I hated the smile on my father's face when he made me do it or when he did it himself. I hated it all.*

There were other things that my father hated. He hated that his father drank—ironic, considering the amount of alcohol and drugs my father consumed in a lifetime. Or maybe that explained my father.

He hated his father's eruptions of rage, some of them predictable, the result of too much drink, and some of them—the worst of them—seemingly without warning.

He hated his mother's begging: *Please, Christophe, don't hurt the boy. Please, Christophe.* So many pleases.

And he hated himself. That was the worst thing to read, but there it was in my father's clumsy, blocky handwriting. *All the guns, all the knives, it would have been so easy. He kept them locked. He kept everything locked. The guns, the knives, the food. But I could have done it. I could have saved her.*

I leaf through all the notebooks after that, trying to find the answer: Save her from what? From whom?

But there is nothing about her. All I can do is wonder: exactly how did my grandmother die?

I set the notebooks aside. I tell myself that I don't know what I'm going to do with them, but that's not true. I am going to keep them. I am going to take them to Aunt Jenny's with me. I will never destroy them.

Twenty-Three

FINN

There are no butterflies in my stomach as I approach her place this time. There's no wondering if I'm doing the right thing. I bound up the front steps and hammer on the door. I keep right on hammering until I see her frowning face peek through the little square of glass.

She's still frowning when she opens the door.

"What are you—?" she begins.

But I push past her into the house. I don't apologize for being rude. I don't apologize for shoving her out of the way so roughly and abruptly that she almost loses her balance. No, I just start right in on her.

"Who are you?" I yell. "Who the hell are you? Why were you at my stepmother's funeral? Why were you at the police station? And my father's club?" She looks surprised at the last question. "I know you were there. I know you talked to Dodo. You were asking about Tracie. Why?"

For someone whose place has been invaded by a hostile force—me—she's remarkably calm. And sad. That throws me a little. She looks so sad.

"I wasn't asking about Tracie," she says.

But I'm not listening. I don't want to hear what she has to say, not until *I* finish what *I* have to say. I'm standing there in the bare dingy foyer to her pathetic little apartment, ready to lambaste her again, when I see papers all over the battered coffee table. I see a name in big print on the top of one of them—*Angela Fairlane Newsome.*

"That's my mother!" I shout at her. I stride into the room and grab the papers and scan them. "What is all of this?" I wave the papers at her. "What are you doing with all this stuff about my family? Who are you?"

She comes into the living room and gently pulls the papers from my hands. She straightens them out so that they're all lined up. She's staring at me in a way that kind of spooks me. What if she's crazy, some psycho chick who maybe has a nice sharp ax tucked away behind the living room door? You never know, right?

"I'm Lila Ouimette," she says.

I stare at her. She's saying it like it's supposed to mean something to me, but it doesn't.

At first.

Then it kicks in.

Ouimette.

"The man who killed my mother—"

"Was my father," she says.

I'm still for a moment. Still, as in stunned to a standstill. As in can't think, can't process the words. Can't believe them. Don't want to believe them. But I'm looking at her, and I see she's waiting for a reaction. Bracing for it, really, like she's expecting some kind of explosion.

And I feel it rising in me, the fuse already lit and burning down. Then the blast happens deep inside me. All I have to do is open my mouth to let it out.

"Your father?" I'm bellowing at her now. "Your father *murdered* my mother?"

I step toward her, my hands tight fists at my side at first, but coming up like a boxer's fists, ready to take that first swing, ready to get the fight started, get the show on the road, ready to do some damage.

"Your father murdered my mother!" I shout the words at her over and over, like I still can't believe it or, maybe, like I want her to show shame, I want her to show me that she has no right to even look at me, let alone talk to me. Who the hell does she think she is?

I'm so close to her that I can feel her breath on my face. It's coming fast in little gasps. She doesn't look scared, but those little puffs of air give her away. Still, she doesn't turn and run. She doesn't even back up.

"I should have told you who I was," she says. "My father—"

The whole place, the walls, the door, the crappy furniture, even her face, is suddenly awash in red, thick and vibrant, like blood. I lash out with my fist—except that at the last minute I uncurl it so that when I hit her, it's a slap. But, still, it's full-force, a resounding slap that sends her reeling so that she has to thrust out a hand against the wall to steady herself. She never takes her eyes off me. She raises her hand to her face and touches it.

"I'm sorry," she says. If I were capable of seeing straight, I might have laughed. I hit her, and she apologizes! But I don't see straight. I think, You *should* be sorry.

"You lied to me," I scream at her. Part of me wants to lash out at her again. The rest of me is ashamed at what I've already done. But the shame doesn't block my fury.

"I never lied," she says.

"You didn't tell me who you were."

Her eyes stay on mine. She nods, but the gesture is barely perceptible.

"I was afraid to," she said. "Afraid of what you might think. What you might do."

I stare at the red mark that covers one whole side of her face. She was right to be afraid. My shame grows. I can't believe that I hit a girl.

"I wanted to talk to you," she says. "I wanted to ask you so many questions. But I was afraid."

I'm still breathing hard, but slowly I'm coming back to myself.

"What did you want to ask me?" I manage to say.

"About what happened that night."

"Which night?"

"The night your mother died. And the night your stepmother died."

The way she says it makes me angry all over again.

"She didn't die. Neither of them died. They were murdered. Shot." It takes every scrap of restraint I can muster to stop myself from doing something I know I will regret.

She nods.

"The night your mother was murdered," she says. "Will you tell me about it again?"

"Tell you what?"

"Everything you remember."

"Why?"

"Because I need to know." She says it softly, and I know it's true. She does need to know. Somewhere under all my anger, I can understand. Her father is her father. He was who he was before she was even born. Is she to blame for what he did? No. But the need to know…I can understand that.

"I already told you everything. And I see you've been checking things out on your own." I nod at the sheaf of papers that she has managed to hold on to.

"Please," she says.

I don't want to, but I do it anyway: I launch into the story. I tell her about leaving the house with my father. I tell her about my mother needing a break (but I don't tell her that it was me she needed a break from). I tell her about going with my dad to his office and spending the night there fooling around. I tell her about my father scooting me out into the hall while he called my mom (but I don't tell her what I think they might be talking about—me). Instead, I tell her about playing with my remote-control cars out there until my dad finally took me upstairs to eat.

She asks me questions, which makes me angry. But then I see the red welt on her face, and I answer. I tell her how long I think I played out in the hallway with the cars. I tell her how long I think we were in the kitchen of the club, eating. I tell her exactly when I found my mother because I can still see the clock on her bedside table.

"What about the security system?" she says.

"What?"

"Your dad had a security system installed just before it happened, right? You told me about it."

"Yeah."

"They say my dad got in because he knew the code," she says.

"They do?"

She looks surprised.

"Don't they?" she asks.

I realize I don't know, and I tell her that.

"My dad didn't tell me any details," I say. "No one did." And I know why: because I fell apart. Because I could barely function. Because I had to go into therapy.

Because I didn't ask.

Because I was weak.

"That's what they say," she says. "Did you see a manual from the security company in your dad's office?"

I'm about to say no. But then I remember.

"He told me some guys were coming to the house to install it," I say.

"But did he have a manual, you know, about how to operate it?"

"I've seen one," I say. "My dad keeps stuff like that in his office. I think he's the only person I know who actually reads manuals. He has one for the phone system, for the computer system, for the accounting software— you name it."

"So you've seen it." She's breathing a little faster now.

"Yeah."

"What does it look like?"

"What do you mean?"

"What does it look like? Does it have a big picture on it? Is it one of those things like they have for that furniture you assemble? You know, they're all pictures so that it doesn't matter what language you speak. You just look at the pictures and you understand?"

"It's an expensive security system, not an IKEA bookshelf," I say.

"What does it look like?"

She's starting to drive me crazy now. What does a manual have to do with anything?

"What does it matter?"

"Please, Finn?"

I don't know why, but I'm surprised she remembers my name. I'm surprised, too, by how I feel when she says it. I like it.

"It's like a book, only with a paper cover. It's filled with fine print in about ten different languages. There are a couple of diagrams inside, you know, with arrows pointing at them. But it's practically impossible to understand. It's written in that crazy English—it sounds like it was originally Japanese or something, and someone ran it through one of those online translation sites."

She nods.

"What about the night your stepmother was killed?" she asks.

I notice that she doesn't say "the night my father killed your stepmother," and it makes me angry all over again.

"What do you want?" I say. "Why are you asking me all these questions?"

"Just tell me what you saw."

"I've already answered a bunch of questions for you. If you want more, first you have to tell me why you want to know all this."

She draws in a deep breath and pulls herself up straight.

"He didn't do it," she says.

What?

"What are you talking about?"

"My father," she says softly. "He didn't do it. He didn't kill your mother."

"I saw him." My voice is loud again. "I saw what he did. I was right in the window the night he killed Tracie. I saw the whole thing."

That shuts her up, but only for a minute.

"He didn't kill your mother," she says. "There's no way—"

My fists curl again. But instead of hitting her, I push past her. I stride out into the hallway, down the stairs, into the street. I do not turn around when she calls my name.

Twenty-Four
LILA

I know what I have to do. I dig in my pocket for a business card and take it to the phone in the kitchen to make a call.

The phone is dead.

Maybe the phone bill is overdue. Maybe the person who lived here before finally cancelled his service. Or maybe he got another phone. Either way, if I want to make a call, I sure can't do it from here.

I lock the door and walk down the street looking for a phone booth. I have to go nearly ten blocks before I find one, and the phone in it isn't working either. I keep walking and finally spot another phone through the window of a Laundromat. I go inside, fish a couple of quarters out of my pocket and punch in the number on the business card.

"Detective Sanders is off today," someone on the other end tells me. "Do you want to leave a message?"

What's the point? She won't be able to call me back. I don't have a phone.

"When is she back in the office?"

"Tomorrow."

"I'll call her back then."

I will call tomorrow. Better, I'll go and see her in person. I'll tell her everything Dodo told me, everything Peter Struthers told me, and what little I know from what Finn said. I'll see what she says.

I leave the Laundromat, then turn and go back inside again, looking for a phone book. There isn't one. So I go to the library instead and wait ten minutes until I can get on the Internet. It's the only way I can think of to get Finn's address.

It takes me forty-five minutes to get to his house by bus and then by walking another dozen or so blocks. They don't run bus routes through the neighborhood where he lives. They don't have to. Everyone there has their own car. And, judging from the size of the garages, I do mean everyone—every man, woman and child.

I find Finn's house. It's big and solid and sits on a small but well-tended lawn neatly bordered by flower beds. I walk up the stone steps and push the button under the intercom next to the big double door.

No one answers.

I push the button again.

Still no answer.

Maybe he isn't home yet. Maybe he went out again. I suddenly realize that this is where my father was killed. That this is the last place he was alive. I want to run, but I can't. I wait.

Half an hour later, I'm ready to go when I see Finn swing around the corner. He's on foot. He has a pizza box in one hand and a slice of pizza in the other. He's wolfing down the slice. He pauses to open the box to pull out another slice but stops when he sees me. He lopes toward me, frowning.

"What are you doing here?"

"I need to tell you something. You left so fast, and I think it's only fair you know…"

"I have nothing to say to you."

"They—the cops—they say my father got the code for your security system from your father's office. Supposedly your father wrote it inside the manual for the alarm system, and my father saw the manual and found the code. They say that's how he got into the house."

"Yeah? So?" He's still angry at me.

"It couldn't have happened that way. You told me yourself that there was no picture on the front of it."

He shoves by me and fishes in his pocket for a key.

"If there was no picture on it, there's no way my father would have known what it was."

He unlocks the front door and steps inside. Only then does he turn to face me.

"What, was he stupid or something?"

What a jerk! But then, what did I expect? What kind of dream world did I think I was living in?

"I didn't have to come here to tell you that," I said. "I just thought you might care. I could have gone straight to the police."

"Right," he says. "Like they're going to believe what you're saying. Like anything you say is going to make a difference."

I tell myself that what happens next is because I'm tired. Tired and discouraged and disappointed—and missing my father. Despite everything, I miss him so much. I miss the life we were going to have together. I feel my cheeks start to burn. Tears well up in my eyes. Angry tears.

"You mean because he's dead, don't you?" I spit the words at him. "You think no one will care because he's dead."

He looks genuinely surprised.

Twenty-Five
FINN

If anyone had ever told me that I would look one day at the daughter of the man who killed my mother and *I* would be ashamed of something I said to her, I would have told that person he was crazy. Certifiably insane. What could I possibly say to the daughter of a murderer that I would ever have to be ashamed of or feel I had to apologize for?

But here I am, standing in the front hall of my own house with exactly that person, the daughter of a murderer, looking right into her eyes and seeing nothing but pain and grief caused by words I have just spoken—and I feel terrible.

"No," I tell her. "No, that's not what I meant."

She's hurt, but she's also full of fire.

"You think it doesn't matter," she says. Tears are trickling down her cheeks. "You think *he* doesn't matter.

You're the only one who's important, is that it? You lost your mother. Well, *I* lost someone too. I lost my father. And I don't care what you or anyone else thinks. I loved him."

I don't doubt her. Not only that, but I don't think she's crazy to say what she's saying. And that's a huge surprise. I guess whenever I thought about it—and I can't say that I gave it much thought—I assumed that everyone in prison was one-hundred-percent screwed up and that the only people who could ever care about them were other criminals.

This girl is not a criminal. She's just a regular girl whose father died the same night Tracie died.

"Well?" she says angrily even while tears trickle down her cheeks. "Aren't you going to say anything?"

I glance across the street and see Mrs. Ashton coming down the walk with her shih tzu. She's looking at me.

"Come in," I tell Lila. I step back to let her pass.

She hesitates, surprised, I think, by the invitation. At first I think she is going to stay put. But when I glance at Mrs. Ashton again, so does Lila, and a cynical little smile twists her lips. She steps in. I shut the door.

"Are you hungry?" I ask.

"No," she says right away, as if she'd have said it no matter what I asked her. But she's looking at the pizza box. I think about her crappy little apartment. I remember the shelves in the kitchen. There was almost nothing there.

"Are you sure?" I say. "Because I have more than I need."

She stares at the pizza box and takes longer to answer this time.

"Maybe one piece," she says finally. She says it like she's doing me a favor.

I flip open the box, and she takes a slice. She takes a tiny bite. The next bite is a lot bigger and, suddenly, she has devoured the whole slice. She glances at me, a look of embarrassment on her face. I hold the box out to her again. She hesitates, but she is staring at the pizza box as if she wants to eat the whole thing.

"Why don't you come and sit down?" I say.

"I should go."

"I thought you wanted to tell me something—about your father."

She follows me into the kitchen. I pull out a couple of plates and some napkins. When I turn around, I see she is gazing around the kitchen, wide-eyed. Our place is nothing like her place.

I put the plates on the table and put another piece of pizza on mine. She glances at me. I nudge the box toward her. She takes a second slice.

"I'm going to have some juice," I say. "You want some?"

She nods. "Please."

We eat the pizza and drink the juice. She looks down at the table the whole time. Finally, when we're done, I wipe my mouth.

"What did you want to tell me about your father?"

She dabs at her mouth with her napkin. Her hands are folded in her lap now. She's studying me, trying to decide. And then she makes up her mind.

She stands up.

"Thanks for the pizza," she says. She turns to go.

I jump to my feet and grab her arm.

"Wait!"

She looks at my hand. I release her. She turns her eyes on me.

"I'm sorry about what I said before. About your dad. Really."

"Right."

There's no way she believes me. Well, really, why do I think she will? You reap what you sow—my Grandma Fairlane used to say that all the time—and with Lila, all I have sowed is anger and hate.

"Please. Sit down. Tell me what you came to tell me."

Our eyes lock. I'm staring at the daughter of my mother's murderer, and I'm thinking that I never in a million years would have thought I could feel what I'm feeling now. There's something about her—the way she holds her head as high as any other girl I know, the way she meets my gaze with grace but also with steel, the strength in her pose that tells me that she's a girl who doesn't give up.

"Please," I say again.

"Why? So you can make fun of my dad again? He was a person, you know. A real person."

"I'm sorry I said that. I want to hear what you have to say."

"You won't like it."

"Tell me anyway."

She sits. So do I.

She stares at the table for a moment as she draws in a deep breath, as if she's gathering herself. Then I'm caught in her eyes again.

"My dad didn't know how to read or write," she says, the words coming out all in a rush. Her eyes are still on me. She's daring me to say something negative about him.

But I'm too busy absorbing what she has just said—and what she has already told me. And what it might mean.

"There's no way he could have known what that manual was," I say. "So how could he have found the code?"

I'm thinking about that manual. I remember it clearly. I remember my dad poring over it. I remember him bugging my mom to read it. I remember thinking I would help her by reading it to her—but when I tried, it didn't make any sense to me. A lot of the words were ones I had never seen or heard before.

"Don't you get it?" she says.

I shake my head. "If he told the cops that—"

"I don't think he did."

"You don't *think*?"

And right there, with those three words, I've lived down to her expectations of me.

"If he'd said he couldn't read, they would have checked it out, right?" she says. "Or are you saying that the ace detectives who nailed him and sent him to prison are all of a sudden incompetent? Or maybe corrupt?"

She pauses a moment, but she's off again before I can get a word in.

"He hid it, okay? He hid it his whole life. He even hid it from me. I only found out after—" Her voice breaks, and she sucks in another deep breath to keep herself from crying again.

She talks for a long time after that, slowly and deliberately. She tells me about a man named Peter Struthers who showed up at her father's funeral. (His funeral… I never even thought about that. She had a funeral to go to, too.) She tells me about the box she found in her father's room and what was in that box. She tells me about Dodo at the club. She tells me what my father wrote in his notebooks, and when she's telling it, I get the impression that she's saying it out loud so that she can make sense of it herself, as if when she read those notebooks, it suddenly occurred to her how little she knew about her father. And then she says:

"If he couldn't read, then there's no way he could have got that code by seeing it in the manual. He wouldn't have known what the manual was. Your dad told the cops he set the alarm when he went out. But the house wasn't broken into, and no alarm went off. Whoever did it must have had the code. But my father didn't. He couldn't have.

Which means that he couldn't have gotten into the
house. He didn't do it. He didn't break into your house.
He didn't—he didn't do the things they said he did."

She means, he didn't kill my mother.

Now it takes me a few moments to gather myself.

"I get that you loved your dad," I say finally. "I can see
it in your eyes when you talk about him. I never thought
about it before, you know, that he had a family and how
his family might feel. I get it now. But—" I hate to be
saying that word. It turns every sentence into its opposite. "But, Lila—" It's the first time I've said her name out
loud. It sounds nice. "They found the stolen jewelry in his
place. It was right there where he was sleeping. If he didn't
do it, how come he had the jewelry?"

"I don't know," she says. "I just know that something's
wrong. My dad knew a lot of people—not nice people,
you know? Maybe one of them did it and framed my dad."

I want to tell her she's crazy. At the very least, she's
grasping at straws.

"If someone wanted to frame your dad for stealing my
mom's jewelry, why would they leave all the jewelry at his
place where the cops could find it? My dad got it all back.
Nothing was missing. If I were going to frame someone,
I'd leave the least valuable pieces to make the cops think
he did it. I wouldn't leave everything."

She is silent for a long time.

"Maybe," she says slowly, her eyes meeting mine
again, "it wasn't about the robbery."

I shake my head right away. I have to. I mean, what she's suggesting is so ridiculous that it's not even worth thinking about, because if it wasn't about the robbery, then the only other thing it could have been about is my mother. She's saying someone *wanted* to kill my mother.

No way.

"Lila," I say. I try to be as understanding as I can. I try not to hurt her, but it's like stabbing someone gently. "Your dad confessed. He told the police he did it. Why would he do that if he was innocent?"

Her shoulders slump, and I actually feel bad that I've taken away all she had left—her belief in her father.

"I don't know," she says.

Then I say something that I regret almost instantly. "He came here. He killed Tracie, and he tried to kill my dad. I know. I saw the whole thing."

She hangs her head, as if she's ashamed.

"That's my fault," she says, her voice so soft I barely catch the words.

"What?"

"It's my fault. He wanted me to go to university. I was supposed to be the first in the family. But I screwed up. I didn't get a scholarship. He came here to get money."

I already knew he wanted money. My dad had told me.

"Did he tell you he was going to do it?" I demand, on edge again. Because if he did, and she didn't say anything...

She shakes her head. "The cops told me—after. I mean, they sort of told me. They asked me if he said anything about needing money. He needed it all right. For me. I guess he thought, well…" She glanced around, making her point. If you want money, a rich man is your best bet. "I'm sorry," she says. "It's all my fault."

She stands up and turns away from me. Her hand goes to her face, and I know she is wiping away her tears before I can see them. Then she spins around. She reaches in her pocket, pulls out some folded papers and throws them onto the kitchen table. They're the articles she printed from the Internet, the ones I saw at her place when I went by the first time. "I have to go," she says. "I have to get things ready for the Salvation Army. I have to call my aunt. I have to go home."

"I'll show you out."

She shakes her head.

"Don't," she says.

"Lila, I—"

She shakes her head again. I watch her walk out of the kitchen. A few moments later, I hear the front door open and close again.

Twenty-Six

FINN

I sit there for a long time staring at the papers but not really seeing them. Instead, I think about Lila. I think about that crappy apartment she's living in and wonder what she meant when she said she had to get things ready for the Salvation Army. Does she mean her dad's things? Is she getting rid of them? There can't even be that much. From what I understand, he was only out of prison for a couple of days before he showed up at our house asking for my dad. I think about what else I saw at her place, which was nothing. There was no sign of anyone else living there. That's when it occurs to me that there isn't anyone else. I have my dad. She has no one.

I start to get up. Something catches my eye. A subheading from one of the articles she printed from the Internet: *Murder weapon never recovered.*

Another piece of information I never knew—or asked about. I drop back down into my chair and reach for the papers. I read them slowly, one by one, and a feeling comes over me: What kind of person am I that I never read all this stuff before now? What kind of son am I? Okay, so I freaked out when it happened. I was seven. What seven-year-old wouldn't have freaked out? And I'm pretty sure my dad did whatever he could to shield me from thinking about that night. Why wouldn't he? I had nightmares for years. I was in therapy. I was a messed-up kid for a long time. But still…

The articles she printed cover a lot of ground. There's information about the actual break-in and shooting, including the information that I was the one who found her. There's information about the arrest and about the suspect, Louis Ouimette, who, according to one article, was known to police and was a reputed small-time thief and drug addict. It is noted that Ouimette worked at my dad's club. There's even a quote from my dad on the subject: "We thought we were doing the right thing when we offered a second chance to the man. I believe in second chances. I still do. I'm only sorry that he let us down."

There's a small article, just a couple of paragraphs:

Fairlane Heiress Murderer Confesses
Louis Ouimette, 35, a reported drug addict with a criminal
record, confessed today to police that he broke into the home
of Robert Newsome and Angela Fairlane Newsome, 30,

*heiress to the Fairlane family fortune, and shot Mrs. Newsome
dead in the course of a robbery.*

*Police believe that Ouimette, who worked at a nightclub
owned by Mr. Newsome, gained access to security codes to the
Newsome house that Mr. Newsome kept in his office. They say
that Ouimette originally claimed to be under the influence
of drugs that night and did not remember anything about
either the break-in or the shooting, but that he confessed in
the face of irrefutable evidence of his involvement in the form
of jewelry stolen from Mrs. Newsome.*

Another brief article: *Fairlane Heiress Murderer Pleads
to Manslaughter, Sentenced to Ten Years.*

Manslaughter?

I read the article.

*In the absence of a murder weapon and proof that Louis
Ouimette acted alone and was the one who pulled the trigger
of the gun that killed Mrs. Angela Fairlane Newsome, heir to
the Fairlane family fortune, the Crown attorney has agreed
to a plea of manslaughter. Ouimette has been sentenced to
ten years on that charge and five years each on the break-
and-enter and theft, all sentences to run concurrently.*

There are a couple of articles, too, on my mother's
family. Her mother passed away the year I was born, when
Mom was only twenty-three. Her father died a year later.
One of the articles was about how my grandfather had

made his fortune. Another one was a long article from a business magazine following his death. According to that article, my mother was going to come into a lot of money one day.

I sigh and get up. This whole thing is giving me a headache.

Then I think about Lila and about everything she's been through. I'm not mad at her for what happened, even though she probably thinks I am. Sure, I hated her at first. But now I can see she was hurt by everything, just like I was. I can see she's just trying to make sense of it all. And I can sure see that she loved her dad, even if I don't quite understand that part of it. It takes a lot to love a dad who, the minute he's out of prison, decides, even for a good reason, to rob someone at gunpoint and ends up shooting someone. But then, I never met the man. All I know is his reputation. Maybe his brain was scrambled by all those drugs.

On the other hand, he learned to read and write.

I put the pizza plates and the juice glasses into the dishwasher. When I straighten up, I glance out the kitchen window. From where I am, I have a perfect view of the front of the garage, and I think back to the night Tracie died. Was shot.

I think about earlier that night too, when a stranger, who turned out to be Lila's dad, came to the house looking for my dad. Maybe if I'd called my dad... But what would I have told him? "There was a man here who wanted to see you." But what man? He didn't give me a name. And if I'd asked, what are the chances that he would have said Louis Ouimette? No, he would have given me a made-up name. He wouldn't have wanted my dad to have any warning.

Great, I've convinced myself that none of what happened was my fault.

I go upstairs. I'm about to flop down on my bed when I catch sight of a piece of paper sticking out from one of my schoolbooks.

It's the bill I found stuck between drawers in Tracie's closet. What was it doing there? Did she toss it there one day when she was in a rush? Or was it there for some other reason? I pull it out and take another look at it. This time I zero in on the date, which confuses me even more. My mom was still alive when this bill was issued. So how come Tracie had it?

I think about what Lila told me. I think about all the things I know now that I didn't know back then. I think about the questions raised by everything that's new to me.

Slowly, as if I'm walking in my sleep, I go to my computer, sit down, and boot it up. I type in the address on the invoice. I grab a jacket, my keys and the papers Lila left. I leave the house.

Twenty-Seven
LILA

When I get back to the apartment, there's a note on the door. The Salvation Army truck has been by, and I missed it. The note tells me it will come by again later, which is fine with me.

I let myself in. I head directly to the kitchen to put the kettle on. While I wait for it to boil, everything that I've been holding back comes flooding out. I weep until my tears dry up, my head aches and my eyes are so puffy I can barely see out of them.

I should call Aunt Jenny. I should tell her that I'm coming home.

But I'm so tired. I turn the kettle off without making tea and instead lie down on the couch.

Twenty-Eight
FINN

Althaus and Son is in the east end of the city on a dreary street that runs off one of the main drags. On one side of the street is a tavern, a burger joint and a U-Store-It facility. On the other side stand a couple of tired houses and, wedged into the end of the street just before the railroad tracks, what looks like a lumberyard but isn't. I pull my car up in front of it and get out. I walk past the stacked wood to the small building in the middle of the lot. I knock on the door.

No one answers.

I try the doorknob. It turns, so I go in.

Right away I see that the little building is well-maintained and spotless inside. There are tools everywhere, but they are all neatly hung on the walls or sit in big, wheeled toolboxes. There's a desk, also spotless; a filing cabinet;

a big table that looks like it's used for drafting. There's also a small counter with a computer and a bell on it.

I ring the bell.

A man appears through a door. As the door opens and closes, I can see through it to a large workshop. Clearly the small building isn't as small as it appeared from the outside. The man wipes his hands on a rag and looks at me.

"Can I help you?"

"I—I need some information."

The man—sandy-haired, stout, middle-aged—waits.

"It's about some work that was done at a nightclub. The Siren."

Recognition flickers in his eyes, but he shakes his head.

"We never did any work there," he says.

"Yes, you did. About ten years ago."

He tosses the rag on the counter and shakes his head again, but now I see irritation in his face.

"I don't know where you're getting your information, kid," he says, "or even why it's any of your business, but I'm telling you, we never did any work at The Siren, and I should know. I've been working here since I was eighteen years old."

I'm guessing he's Althaus's son.

"Maybe your father—" I begin, but he cuts me off with a wave of his hand.

"My dad passed," he says.

"I'm sorry."

He grunts, appreciative, I think, of the sentiment. I pull the invoice out of my pocket, unfold it and hand it to him.

He squints at it, crosses to his desk and pulls a pair of glasses out of a drawer. He puts them on and studies the invoice.

"Well, that's us, all right," he says, looking up at me. "And that's my dad's handwriting." He looks at the invoice again. "Looks like he wrote this just before…" He clears his throat. "He died not long after he wrote this. Cancer."

"I'm sorry," I say again.

He hands the invoice back to me.

"I don't know anything about this," he says. "And even if I did, I still don't see how it's any business of yours."

"My dad owns The Siren," I say.

The man looks me over again.

"They were planning a big renovation about ten years ago," he said. "They put out a request for bids. My dad bid on the job. It was a fair price. Maybe not as cheap as some, but my dad was a real craftsman. You paid, but you always got better quality than you paid for. We didn't get the job. And, anyway, if we had got it—" He has to draw in a deep breath to compose himself. "He would never have been able to handle something that big. His health was failing. He died a few months later."

"But he did *some* work there," I say. "I was hoping you could tell me what it was."

He sticks out his hand, and I give him the invoice again. He shakes his head.

"There's not much detail here," he says. In fact, there's none. Nothing but a price.

The door behind him opens again, and a woman comes in.

"Charlie, that woman called—" She stops short when she sees me. "Oh. I didn't know there was anyone here with you."

"It's okay, Mom." He glances at the invoice again and then holds it out to her. "You know anything about this?" he asks her. To me he says, "Mom handles the books."

She scans the paper and looks up in surprise.

"That's the second time someone has asked me about this."

Charlie Althaus and I both stare at her.

"Someone else asked you about the same invoice?" Charlie asks.

"A woman. The wife of the man your father did the work for."

"A blond?" I ask.

"Dad did work for The Siren?" Charlie says. "But our bid was rejected."

"Yes, a blond," Mrs. Althaus says. It was Tracie. My mother had chestnut hair. "And yes, that bid was rejected.

But the club owner called your father. I think he felt badly that he was ill. He had a little job he needed done. It wasn't much, but I think your father was glad to be asked. It wasn't long after that that he was in the hospital."

Charlie looks perplexed.

"How come I didn't know about that?"

Mrs. Althaus smiles. "Because you were on your honeymoon with Allison. I didn't even know much about it. It was a small job. You father went in and did it in a couple of days. He didn't talk about it. He was too exhausted when he came home at night. I didn't even remember it until that woman came in with this invoice."

"What was the job?" I ask.

Mrs. Althaus crosses to the filing cabinet. Her knees pop as she bends down to pull out the bottom drawer. Her fingers walk over the tops of the file folders inside until she reaches one about halfway back. She pulls it out and struggles to straighten up again. Charlie has to take her by the hand and help her. She opens the file folder, pulls out a couple of sheets and hands them to Charlie. Charlie studies them and frowns.

"He was doing a whole renovation over there. Why didn't he ask one of those workmen to do this?"

"Do what?" I say.

He passes me the papers. I stare at them.

"Can I have these?" I say.

"I can make you copies, if you'd like," Mrs. Althaus says. "But the originals stay here. I told that other woman the same thing."

"You made copies for her?"

She nods.

* * *

I read the papers a couple of times before I finally fold them up and put them in my pocket. I go straight to the club.

I can tell right away that something is going on. Usually at this time of day, the staff is all there and they're getting ready to open. Today everyone is here. But they're standing around in little groups, talking.

Matthew Goodis spots me on my way through to the stairs that lead to my dad's office. He catches up to me.

"Your dad's not here," he says. He looks upset and distracted.

"That's okay. I just wanted to drop something in his office." I glance at the staff. "What's going on?"

"There was an accident."

"Oh." Then, since he's here, I ask him a question. "You know that renovation you did about ten years ago? Was anything done in my dad's office?"

"What?" He's been checking his watch, probably wanting to break up all the chit-chat and get everyone to work.

"Were any renovations done in my dad's office?"

He shakes his head. "We built up and out. It was a major project. But down where your dad is? No. Why?"

"Nothing at all?"

"Not that I know of. Why? What's up, Finn?"

"Do you remember the night my mom was killed?"

"I remember the phone call from your dad asking me to cut my vacation short."

"You were on vacation?"

"That reno was tough. I put in eighteen-hour days around here. As soon as we reopened, your dad gave me six weeks off. I was four weeks in when he called me with the awful news." He shakes his head again. "I guess you've been thinking about that, huh?"

"Yeah." I change the subject. "I have to leave something for my dad. Is his office unlocked?"

Matthew digs in his pocket and pulls out some keys. He snaps one off and hands it to me.

"Return it on your way out," he says.

I go downstairs and unlock the door to my father's office. I pull out the papers Mrs. Althaus gave me and try to figure them out. Then I go to the wall indicated. But there's nothing there except a couple of shelves and a few pictures.

I stare at the work order again. I start rapping on the wall. *Rap, rap.* Move over a little. *Rap, rap.* Move over a little. *Rap, rap.*

I freeze.

I rap again.

I'm not imagining things.

I look for a crack or a seam, anything. But there's nothing there.

I leave my father's office, locking the door behind me.

I check the room next door. It's a storeroom, with access to the main hall in the basement and to another, smaller, storeroom next door. I want to check that room, but it's locked.

I go upstairs and look for Matthew. He's on the phone. He hangs up just as I reach him and hand him the key.

"Have you talked to your dad in the past couple of hours?" he asks.

"No. Why?"

"I can't raise him on his cell. When you see him, tell him to call me. It's about Dodo."

"Dodo? What's up with him? He didn't quit, did he?" Every now and then Dodo would get fed up with the mess in the bathrooms and threaten that he was through.

"He was the accident I mentioned. Looks like he took a nasty fall."

"Is he okay?"

"Look, Finn…"

"Is Dodo okay, Matthew?"

"He's dead."

Twenty-Nine
FINN

Dodo is dead? I can hardly believe it. He's been around the club forever. I'm pretty sure Dad hired him before I was born. Poor old guy. He was in a car accident awhile back. He almost died. He was in the hospital for months with a caved-in skull. Dad took him back but had to give him a different job. He couldn't be a bouncer anymore.

I'm so shaken up that it takes me a few moments to refocus.

I circle around to the back of the club and walk the length of the alley. I locate the small barred window to my father's office. I walk down the alley from there until I come to another door, which I'm pretty sure is the door to the second storeroom. I stare at it. I try to open it, but, no surprise, it's locked.

When I finally get back into the car, I pull out the papers that Lila left and read through them again. I stop at the one that says the gun was never found. They caught Lila's dad with my mom's jewelry, but they didn't find the gun. If Lila's right, if her dad was set up, then whoever killed my mom must have hidden it. So how did Lila's dad get his hands on it as soon as he got out of prison? There were only a couple of ways I could think of. One, Lila's dad wasn't framed after all; he was smart enough to get rid of the gun but stupid enough to get caught with the jewels. But that didn't make sense. How could one person be that smart about one thing and so spectacularly stupid about another? Two, when he got out of prison, he got the gun from whoever framed him. But who was that person? And why would that person give him the gun? Or had he taken it and killed that person, maybe for revenge? But if he had, wouldn't the cops have found the body by now, and wouldn't they have matched it to the same gun? If they had, they would have told us—wouldn't they?

Neither option made sense.

I flip through more articles. I stop at my grandfather's obituary and skim it again.

One day. I stare at those two words. It says my mother would inherit a lot of money *one day*. Why was it worded that way? My mother was an only child. If her father died, wouldn't she inherit the money right away?

I shove the papers into the glove compartment and get out of the car. I head back into the club. Matthew has managed to get everyone to work. He starts toward me as soon as he sees me.

"Did you get ahold of your dad?" he asks.

I shake my head.

"Can I ask you something, Matthew?"

"Okay, I guess."

"You've worked for my dad for a long time, right?"

"Since the beginning."

"And you knew my mom."

He smiles for a moment. Then his smile fades, and he searches my face. "Why? Are you okay, Finn?"

"I'm fine. Really. I was just wondering...She inherited a lot of money when her father died, didn't she?"

He doesn't answer.

"Didn't she, Matthew?"

"That's probably something you want to talk to your dad about, Finn."

"So you don't know?"

More silence. He knows, all right. He just doesn't want to say.

"We've been having this debate in Social Studies, I say. "About rich guys and what they plan to do with their money. You've read about all those billionaires who plan to give everything to charity and not to their kids, right?"

Matthew laughs. "Are you worried that's what your dad's going to do?"

"No. But I was just wondering...I know my grandfather was pretty well-off."

"*Pretty* well-off? Try loaded. The man had more money than he knew what to do with."

"Did my mom get it all when he died? Or was he one of those guys who thought that if he could make it on his own, his kids should be able to do the same?"

"Naw. He wasn't like that. He doted on your mother."

"So she got everything?"

"I really think that's a question for your dad."

"Come on, Matthew." I sound like a kid trying to wheedle a chocolate bar out of a favorite uncle.

"The deal was she'd get it all when she turned thirty," he says at last.

"She was only twenty-three when he died."

"I guess your granddad thought she'd be better able to handle it when she was older." He peers at me again. "Did someone say something to you? Is that it, Finn?"

I don't answer.

"Whoever it was, whatever they said, it's just talk," he says angrily. "It was garbage when the cops started looking at him. They found that out soon enough. But people talk." He shook his head in disgust. "They talk too much, if you ask me."

"What do you mean, Matthew?"

Matthew is startled when he realizes he's said too much.

"Are you telling me the cops suspected my dad of killing my mom?" I say slowly.

"No. No, I didn't mean—"

"But that's what you said."

"You know what cops are like. They suspect everyone. But they gave it up pretty fast. They had to. You were with your dad the whole time. There was no way he could have gone anywhere without you seeing him—assuming he'd do something so crazy in the first place." He shakes his head again, angered by the memory. "If he hadn't hired that junkie, this never would have happened."

"You mean if *you* hadn't hired him," I say. Matthew does all the hiring. My dad just okays his decisions. That's why the article had referred to "we" deciding to give someone a second chance.

Again, Matthew looks startled. He opens his mouth to say something and then clamps it shut again.

I'm getting a weird feeling. I've known Matthew forever. I know when something's wrong.

"Yeah," he says. "Look, Finn..."

"You did hire him, didn't you, Matthew?"

"Yeah," he says again. But he sounds angry and maybe a little nervous. "I just said I did, didn't I? I have to get back to work."

"Dad said you knew about him before you hired him," I say.

Matthew tenses.

"Did you?" I press.

"Yeah," he says. "Like your dad said."

"Then why did you hire him?" I'm almost yelling, and I don't know why. What does it matter? It's in the past.

A cell phone trills. Matthew reaches into his pocket, pulls out his phone and checks the display. "I have to take this, Finn. But, listen, talk to your dad, okay? He'll explain it all to you."

I go back to the car and start the engine. Then I shut it off again. I don't know what to do or who to talk to. While I'm sitting there, Matthew comes out of the club. He doesn't see me. He gets into his car and roars away.

I take out my phone. After a few moments, I punch in Lila's number.

An automated voice tells me that that number is no longer in service. Has she left town already?

I decide to find out.

I head for her apartment.

Thirty
LILA

I wake up with a start. The flat is dark. I thrust out my wrist to check the time, but it's too dark to read my watch. I stand up and grope for a light. When I find it and flip it on, I gasp.

There's a man in the apartment.

He's dressed in a black coat over black pants. He's wearing black gloves and has a balaclava over his head.

He's holding a gun.

His voice is low and menacing when he says, "Don't scream. Don't make a sound."

I'm shaking all over. I can't believe this is happening. I don't understand why it's happening.

"There's nothing here," I say. "I don't have any money. There's nothing to steal."

"Lie down on the floor," he says. "Facedown."

I start to do what he tells me. But I stop when I am
on my knees. If I lie down, I will be totally at his mercy.
Besides, I'm sure he's in the wrong place.

"I said, lie down," he says, his voice rumbling like
a rock slide.

"You've the got wrong place," I say again. "Please.
Just look around—"

"I'm not going to tell you again," he says. He points
the gun straight at me. The barrel is only a few inches from
my head. That's when I realize that he doesn't care what is
or isn't in the apartment. He isn't here to take anything.
No, he's completely crazy. A psycho. He probably doesn't
even care that someone will hear the gunshot—assuming
any of my neighbors (none of whom I know) will hear
or, if they do, that they'll know what it was, and if they
recognize the sound, that they'll do anything about it.

I lie down. He plants a foot on my back and brings
his full weight down on me as he bends over. I feel
like my ribs are going to collapse under his weight.
He fastens my hands together with restraints that are
like the plastic strips that come with trash bags, but
thicker, longer and stronger. His foot is still on my back,
but most of his weight is on the floor now, although
I know that will change quickly if I struggle. He pulls
something out of his pocket. It's a roll of duct tape.
He rips off a piece, leans down again and presses the
tape over my mouth.

His foot leaves my back. He grabs the plastic that's binding my wrists and drags me over to the radiator against the wall. He uses another restraint to bind me to the radiator.

"There," I hear him say. "Now be a good girl and stay put while I get your things together."

I twist my head around. Over my shoulder, I see him leave the room.

As soon as he's gone, I start to pull against the plastic. The pain is searing where the bands slice into my wrists. But I don't stop. I pull, I writhe, I twist. All I succeed in doing is cutting deeper into my flesh.

I hear him moving around. I see him come out of the little hall where the bedrooms are. He has a small duffel bag and a backpack in his hand. My duffel bag. My backpack. He goes through the kitchen to the back door. I hear it open. He's taking my things. But why?

I freeze.

What if he comes back and takes me next? What if he loads me and my things into his car or his truck or his van—whatever he has out there—and he drives me far away, into the woods or to some abandoned building somewhere? What if he…?

I've told everyone I'm going back to Aunt Jenny's— everyone, that is, except Aunt Jenny. Aunt Jenny isn't expecting to see me for another six weeks. And anyone here who might look for me—Detective Sanders is the only person I can think of—will think I've headed home. She's already told me the case is closed. She won't be looking for me either. I didn't even leave my name the last time I called her. I just told the person who answered the phone that I'd try again.

This man could take me and do whatever he wants with me and no one will even miss me—not until it's too late.

I feel panic flood through me. I can't move. And even if I could, what then?

But I have to do something. He'll be back any minute. He'll be free to do whatever he wants.

I struggle again, and the plastic cuts so deep into my wrists that I feel the blood, warm and sticky. But I don't stop.

Someone knocks on the front door.

The Salvation Army.

I try to scream, but the sound that comes out is dry and hoarse and barely audible.

So I raise both my legs high into the air and bring them down fast, crashing my heel against the floor. The impact jars my legs. But the sound—a reverberating thud—is gratifying.

I hear another knock at the door.

I bring my legs up again and slam my heels again and again.

"Hello?" a voice calls from outside. "Is everything okay in there?"

I keep slamming my heels down, harder and harder, faster and faster.

But when I stop, I hear only silence. Then I hear: "Lila?"

A moment later, I hear the front doorknob rattle.

I keep on banging.

I hear something slam against the door. I hear it again, followed by another sound—the door's flimsy lock has given way. Someone appears. I see his face in the backlit gloom.

Finn.

He stares down at me in astonishment. Then he comes toward me and kneels down. He's so busy trying to figure out how to free me that he doesn't see or hear what I do. He doesn't see the man with the gun come back through the kitchen.

At least, I don't think he sees.

But as the man raises the hand with the gun, ready, I think, to smash Finn with it, Finn goes still and peers into my eyes. Maybe it's the terror he sees there that makes him suddenly turn.

The man with the gun freezes—but just for a moment. Then he lunges forward, hand raised again.

Just before the man reaches him, Finn rolls away from me.

Surprised, the man crashes to the ground. The gun falls from his grip.

Finn sees it and makes a grab for it.

The man dives on top of Finn. I want to help Finn. I want to do something. But I am still firmly attached to the radiator.

The man punches Finn, and Finn flies backward again. Before he can recover, the man has the gun and is on his feet. He's waving the gun at Finn, his voice even deeper now as he tells him to get over by the radiator. He steps back a little out of Finn's reach as Finn struggles to a sitting position. The man has forgotten all about me, but I haven't forgotten about him.

He's out of Finn's reach, but he's close to me now. I pull my legs back a little and then kick out with them as hard as I can, my feet striking him just behind his knees.

The man's knees buckle involuntarily. As he struggles to regain his balance, he drops the gun again. Finn lunges for it, grabs it and jumps to his feet. He's pointing the gun at the man now.

"Stay down," he says.

The man doesn't move.

Finn backs over to where I am. He keeps the gun and his eyes on the man as he reaches back and pulls the tape from my mouth.

"Are you okay?" he says.

I nod. Then I realize he still isn't looking at me. He's too intent on the man.

"I'm okay," I say.

Finn stands where he is. I realize he isn't sure what to do now. I'm still tied up, but the man on the floor isn't.

"Get up," Finn says to the man.

The man staggers to his feet.

"Hands above your head," Finn says.

The man raises his hands slowly.

"Keep your hands up and put them against the wall," Finn says.

The man hesitates.

"Do it," Finn roars.

The man does as he's told.

"Now step back," Finn says. "But keep your hands on the wall."

The man steps his feet back.

"Farther," Finn says.

The man steps back farther until his feet are more than a meter away from the wall. His hands are still on the wall. Finn approaches him from behind. If the man tries anything, all Finn has to do is kick the man's feet away and the man will drop to the floor.

Finn reaches for the man's coat pocket.

The man starts to turn.

Finn jabs the gun into his back. The man goes still. Finn pats the pockets of the man's coat. He pats one side of the man's pants, then the other. He reaches into a pants pocket and pulls out a set of keys. Attached to them is a jackknife. Finn stares at it, very still.

"Stay put," Finn tells the man. His voice is hoarse now. He steps away from the man, still watching him closely, and backs up until he gets to me. With one hand, he opens the knife, squats down and slices through the plastic bands.

I sit up.

"Are you okay?" Finn says.

I nod. "He broke in here. I don't even know what he wants. We have to call the police," I say.

Finn glances at me. That's when the man makes a move. He turns around. My whole body tenses.

Finn raises the gun.

"I'll shoot," he says. "If you don't believe me, try me."

The man stops. For the first time since I first saw him, he seems unsure of himself.

Thirty-One
FINN

The whole way over to Lila's place, I'm trying to reach my dad. But he must have shut off his phone.

When I knock on Lila's door, there is no answer. Then I hear a crash. And another crash.

That's when I look into the front window and see her lying on the floor, tied somehow to the radiator in the living room. There's a frantic look on her face. I don't even think about it. I break down the door.

I start to free her when I see terror in her eyes. Someone is behind me. Just like that, I find myself in a fight with a man with a gun. Nothing like this has ever happened to me before. My first reaction: No way. There is no way this is really happening. No way the gun is real.

But the guy comes at me like the only thing on his mind is killing me.

It *is* real.

He gets the better of me. He's holding the gun on me and telling me to get down. I'm staring at that gun. I'm thinking, so this is what it feels like to stare death in the face. It's a cold feeling. A numb feeling. My mouth goes dry. As I stare at the gun, it seems to get bigger and bigger until the man standing in front of me is holding a cannon, pointed at me.

Then Lila kicks out with both feet and the man goes down.

I'm still not sure exactly when it all comes together. Is it the grunt when he hits the floor? Is it the way he moves when he struggles to his feet at my command and plasters his hands to the wall? Then, when I'm searching him, I reach into his pocket and find a clump of keys. I pull it out. There's a knife attached to the key ring— a Swiss Army knife. I feel like I've been kicked in the stomach, but I keep my eyes on him. I keep the gun on him too, as I back carefully toward Lila and reach down with my left hand to slice through her plastic restraints.

She tells me she's okay. She sits up. Her wrists are bleeding, but I don't ask her about them. My eyes, my mind, my whole being is focused on the man with his hands still plastered to the wall. He obeys me for a while. Then, even after I threaten to shoot him, he twists his head around and watches me.

I say, "Take the mask off, Dad."

Lila is on her feet behind me.

"Dad?" she says.

The man doesn't move.

"Do it," I say, "or I'll do it for you."

The man reaches up slowly with one hand and pulls the balaclava off his head. There he is, hair sticking up, face red from the heat—my dad.

Lila stares open-mouthed at me.

"My phone is in my pocket," I tell her. "Take it and call nine-one-one."

"Finn, I can explain," my dad says. My dad, who a few minutes before was locked in combat with me.

"He put all my stuff in a car out back," Lila says. She has my cell phone in her hand. "He was going to kill me."

I stare at him, and I feel like I'm staring at a complete stranger who only happens to look like my father.

"Call the cops," I say to Lila. "Do it now."

"Finn, wait." My father's hands come off the wall and he turns around. He starts toward me.

I raise the gun. "Don't, Dad. I mean it."

He stops. He puts his hands up in the air.

"It's not what you think, son," he says.

"You killed my father, and you were going to kill me," Lila says.

"Your father killed my wife," my father says. "He killed both of my wives."

I can't believe how pathetic he is.

"Her father didn't kill Mom," I say. "There was no way he could have found that security code. He was framed."

My father stares at me. I see he is thinking.

"It was Tracie," he says finally. "I didn't know what she was doing. I swear I didn't. She wanted your mother out of the way."

"Tracie? You're blaming all of this on Tracie?"

My dad hangs his head. I think he's trying to show me how ashamed he is.

"We were—Finn, your mom and I weren't getting along. Then I did something stupid. I met Tracie and—"

What? "Is that why Mom wanted a break that night?"

My dad nods.

"You said that was my fault. You said she wanted a break from me."

"I'm sorry, son. I—I didn't know what else to say. But I swear I had nothing to do with killing her. That was Tracie. I had no idea. Then when she found out that Ouimette was getting out of prison, she got in touch with him. She was blackmailing me. She said if I didn't do what she wanted, she would go to the cops and tell them I was the one who was responsible for what happened to your mother. She said Ouimette would back her up. She said he'd do anything if she paid him enough. It wasn't like they could send him back to prison if he said I hired him to do it. He'd already done his time."

I glance at Lila again. I don't know what she's thinking.

"Why would Tracie blackmail you?"

"She wanted out of the marriage, and she wanted half of everything I had."

Half of everything you had thanks to Mom, I thought.

"So you're telling me that Lila's dad came to the house because Tracie was going to pay him to help her blackmail you? Is that what you're saying, Dad?"

My dad glances at Lila. He nods.

"Even though he had nothing to do with killing Mom?"

"What are you talking about, Finn? The man confessed," my dad says.

"He didn't do it, Dad. He couldn't have done it. I know it, and Lila knows it. And I bet he knew it too. Isn't that right, Dad? Isn't that why he wanted to talk to you?"

"I don't know where you got that idea, Finn. I just told you—"

"He came to the house and he asked for you. Not Tracie. You. You know what I think, Dad? I think he figured out what happened. I think he came to the house to tell you that. Maybe he was threatening to go to the police. Or maybe he just wanted money. And you know what else I think?"

He didn't answer.

"I think you used the opportunity to get rid of them both. You had the gun that you used to kill Mom. You lunged at him and made it look like he killed Tracie."

"You think I killed Tracie? Why would I do that?"

"Because she knew about the secret door in your office. She knew you killed Mom. Maybe she was blackmailing you, but if she was, it was because she found out what you did. She had proof. So you killed her, and then you killed Lila's dad. With them both dead, you were in the clear. That's the way you had it figured, right, Dad?"

"No. No, that's not what happened. I told you. It was Tracie. I think she wanted him to kill me. He pulled that gun, and I struggled with him. That's when it went off and killed Tracie." He breaks off for a moment, overcome by emotion, although I can't say which one. "I'm sorry, Finn. I had no idea it was her. I didn't even suspect until she told me she wanted a divorce."

"If that's what really happened, why didn't you tell all that to the cops?" I ask.

"Because I wanted to put it behind me. I wanted to put it behind *us*, Finn. Tracie got what she deserved. It was over. I didn't want to dredge up everything that happened ten years ago. I didn't want to put you through that. And I guess I didn't want you to think less of me—if I'd been smarter ten years ago, I never would have got involved with Tracie, and maybe none of this would have happened."

I glance at Lila. She's glowering at my dad. She doesn't believe a word he's saying.

"Call the cops," I tell her.

"But Finn, son…" my dad says.

"If you didn't do anything wrong, Dad, then you have nothing to worry about," I tell him. "But you have to tell the cops what you just told me."

"What's done is done, son. No matter what happens now, your mother is never going to come back."

"Make the call," I say again. This time I shout the words at her.

She lifts the phone.

My dad hurls himself across the room at her.

The gun goes off.

My dad falls to the floor.

I stare at the gun in my hand.

I hear Lila talking into the phone. She's giving her address. She's saying, "Someone has been shot."

Thirty-Two
LILA

Finn is standing in my living room, staring at his father. A gun hangs limply in his hand. After I finish my call, I put the phone down and go to his father. I press two fingers to the side of his neck to feel his pulse.

"He's alive," I say.

His father groans.

"There are a couple of clean towels in a box on the kitchen table. Get them," I say.

Finn doesn't move.

"Go," I tell him. "We have to stop the bleeding."

He walks slowly from the room, the gun still hanging from his right hand. I'm not sure where he's going, but a moment later he is back with the clean dish towels in his hand. He gives them to me. I fold them into a thick pad and press it down hard on Robert Newsome's chest.

Finn stands off to one side, watching. He doesn't say a word.

Pretty soon I hear an ambulance siren. I hear car doors open and slam shut. Then silence. Then more car doors. Someone calls into the house:

"Police. We're coming in."

I glance at Finn, who is still holding the gun.

"Put it down," I say.

But too late. Cops appear in Kevlar vests and what looks like full assault gear. They see the gun in Finn's hand and start yelling at him to put it down and to get down on his knees with his hands clasped behind his head. I try to tell them that he's not the one, but all they see is the gun. Who can blame them? They have no idea what went on here. For all they know, Finn could be dangerous.

Finn doesn't move. The cops are all pointing their guns at him. Their faces are tense.

"Finn," I say quietly. "It's over. Put it down."

He blinks. He turns and looks at me. He looks down at the gun in his hand. Then, as if for the first time, he sees the cops. Slowly he raises one hand over his head. He bends slowly at the knees and lays the gun on the floor. He raises his other hand. The cops yell at him again to get down on his knees and clasp his hands behind his head. He obeys, and they swarm toward him and handcuff him. Someone calls "All clear," and the paramedics arrive. They ask me what happened. I tell them, and they take over.

The cops are all over me too, checking to make sure I don't have a gun, asking me for my name. I tell them I want to talk to Detective Sanders, Homicide. They look surprised, but someone relays the message. The next thing I know, they are taking me into the kitchen and telling me to sit down at the table. One of them starts asking me questions. He wants to know who the victim is, who the shooter is, what happened. After the paramedics stabilize Finn's father, one of the cops gets one of them to look at my wrists. The paramedic puts antiseptic on them and bandages them. He tells me to have a doctor look at them.

It isn't long before Detective Sanders and her partner arrive. I watch her face while she is briefed by one of the first cops on the scene. I see the intensity in her eyes as she takes in the scene around her. She comes toward me, looking for a moment at the bandages on my wrists. The very first thing she says is, "Are you okay, Lila?" I nod.

"Where's Finn?" I ask.

"They took him in. Lila, I need you to tell me what happened."

I start talking, beginning with waking up and seeing a stranger with a gun in my house. I tell her that he took my things and put them outside, in a car, I think. She nods. I tell her about Finn showing up and what happened after that. Then I'm looping back to my first meeting with Finn and then back again to Dodo and, before that, Peter Struthers.

I seem to talk forever. She listens without interrupting. Only when I finally stop does she begin her questions. She wants me to tell her some things again. She wants more information about other things. She starts writing things down. Finally she says, "We should get your wrists looked at. Then I'll need you to give a formal statement. Okay?"

Detective Sanders takes me to the hospital, where a doctor eventually looks at my wrists and tells me there may be scars. I don't care.

Then I make my statement.

When I've finished, someone whispers something in Detective Sanders's ear.

"Your aunt is on her way here," she says. "We're going to get you a room somewhere until she gets here. If you want someone to stay with you, we can do that too."

I tell her I'll be fine.

"What about Finn?" I say. "Where is he?"

"He's outside."

"Is he under arrest?"

She shakes her head.

"Can I see him?"

She shows me where he's sitting, which is exactly where he was sitting the first time I saw him, when I had no idea who he was. I drop down into the chair next to his. He doesn't even look at me.

"I heard your dad's going to be okay," I say after a few moments.

He is silent. I think maybe he doesn't want to talk to me. I think maybe he blames me for everything that's happened.

Then he speaks.

"He killed my mom."

I decide to wait.

"She had just inherited a lot of money from her father. A *lot*," he says. "He didn't want to let all that money slip away from him. It's probably why he married her in the first place."

What can I say to that?

"He got away with killing her because of me," he says. "Because I was right there with him the whole time. He knew she was already dead before we even left the club that night. He killed her. But he took me home and let me go upstairs alone." He turns his head, and I see tears. "He let me go upstairs even though he knew she was up there. He let me find her."

I want to touch him. I want to hold his hand, but I don't dare.

"He used me. And he used your dad. He hired your dad even though he knew all about his problems. He told me Matthew hired him, but he didn't. My dad hired your dad so that he could use him. He used him twice. He framed him for my mom's murder. Then he got him to come to the house, and he made it look like he killed Tracie."

And then he killed my dad, I think. But I don't say it.

"Tracie found out what he'd done. She found an old bill for some work he'd had done at the club. She found out what it was for. He'd had a secret door put in so he could get out of his office that night to kill my mother. My dad was telling the truth about at least a part of it—Tracie was using that bill as leverage to get a good settlement from my dad. She really did want half of everything. And for that, he wanted to get rid of her. That's why your father came to the house that night. My dad told me that your father called him. He did, too. But it wasn't his idea to come to our house. That was my dad's idea. My dad told your dad to meet him at the house. He set it all up. And I was his witness—again."

"He had no way of knowing you would see," I say softly.

Finn's eyes are hard. "Maybe. But he knows me pretty well. He knew I was up in my room. He knew I'd probably be on my computer. I told him I didn't have any plans. He knew what I could see from my window. He knew—"

I hear footsteps. A male voice says, "Finn?"

Finn turns.

"Finn, are you okay?" the man says.

Finn just stares at him, shell-shocked.

Detective Sanders appears.

"Mr. Goodis?" she says.

The man nods.

"May I speak with you for a moment?"

She takes Mr. Goodis inside. Finn stares straight ahead. He stays that way until Mr. Goodis comes back with Detective Sanders.

"Come on, Finn," he says.

* * *

Detective Sanders checks me into a decent motel. She asks me if I'm sure I don't want someone to stay with me. She offers to stay herself. I say no. She leaves me her card and tells me to call if I need anything. Anything at all.

I sit in a chair inside the room and stare out the window until someone knocks on the door, and Aunt Jenny says, "Lila?"

I open the door, fall into her arms and cry. We stand like that for a long time. Aunt Jenny cries too. She listens to everything I say and tells me she's sorry. She says it over and over again. "Lila, I'm so sorry."

Thirty-Three
LILA

Aunt Jenny and I do one last sweep of the room. She wants to make sure that we don't leave anything behind, even though we were only there one night and neither of us has much to lose. I have my duffel bag and my backpack, brought from the flat by Detective Sanders. I also have my father's notebooks and Detective Sanders's card. I know, because I asked, that Robert Newsome will be okay and that he's been charged with three counts of first-degree murder—so far. Detective Sanders says they're looking into what happened to Edward Alonzo.

"Who?" I say.

"He also went by the name Dodo."

I ask about Finn and am told that he is staying with Matthew Goodis, manager of The Siren and the person designated by his mother to be his guardian if anything should happen to both his parents.

Part of me wants to call him or see him before I leave. But the other part, the larger part, resists. I don't want to cause him any more pain. I've already turned his life upside down. If he wants to see me or talk to me, okay. Otherwise…

I keep hoping he'll show up at the motel. When we go downstairs with our things, I hope he might be in the lobby.

He isn't.

When we go outside to get a taxi to the train station, I hope he might be out there, waiting.

He isn't.

The taxi driver puts all of our things into the trunk.

"Come on, Lila," Aunt Jenny says.

I'm about to get into the cab when a car pulls up. I wait, still hoping. But it isn't Finn. It's Matthew Goodis. He nods when he sees me and gives me an envelope.

"Is he okay?" I ask.

Matthew Goodis is direct. "Not really. Not now," he says. "It's going to take time. But he's faced a lot before and came through it."

I nod. I tuck the envelope into my purse and watch him get back into his car and drive away. I don't open it until we are on the train and Aunt Jenny has dozed off.

The envelope contains a sheet of paper. There are exactly two words on it: *I'm sorry*.

I dig in my purse for a pen. I turn the paper over and begin to write back to Finn. I want to tell him that I'm sorry too.

Norah McClintock has written many acclaimed novels. *Taken* won the 2011 Manitoba Young Readers Choice Award and is nominated for the ALA Quick Pick list. Norah lives in Toronto, Ontario.